TIGER MOTH

KUNG POW

CHICKEN

Librarian Reviewer
Katharine Kan
Graphic novel reviewer and Library Consultant, Panama City, FL
MLS in Library and Information Studies, University of Hawaii at
Manoa, HI

Reading Consultant
Elizabeth Stedem
Educator/Consultant, Colorado Springs, CO
MA in Elementary Education, University of Denver, CO

STONE ARCH BOOKS
Minneapolis   San Diego

Graphic Sparks are published by Stone Arch Books
151 Good Counsel Drive, P.O. Box 669
Mankato, Minnesota 56002
www.stonearchbooks.com

Library of Congress Cataloging-in-Publication Data
Reynolds, Aaron, 1970–
Kung Pow Chicken / by Aaron Reynolds; illustrated by Erik Lervold.
p. cm. — (Graphic Sparks—Tiger Moth)
ISBN 978-1-4342-0455-4 (library binding)
ISBN 978-1-4342-0505-6 (paperback)
1. Graphic novels. I. Lervold, Erik. II. Title.
PN6727.R45K86 2008
741.5'973—dc22 2007031253

Summary: Weevil's evil goons have captured Tiger Moth! The fate of this fourth-grade ninja rests in the hands of Kung Pow and his kid sister, Amber. Have Tiger's lessons prepared his young apprentice for this life or death bug battle? Or will Kung Pow fail the ultimate ninja test?

Art Director: Heather Kindseth
Graphic Designer: Brann Garvey

1 2 3 4 5 6 13 12 11 10 09 08

Printed in the United States of America

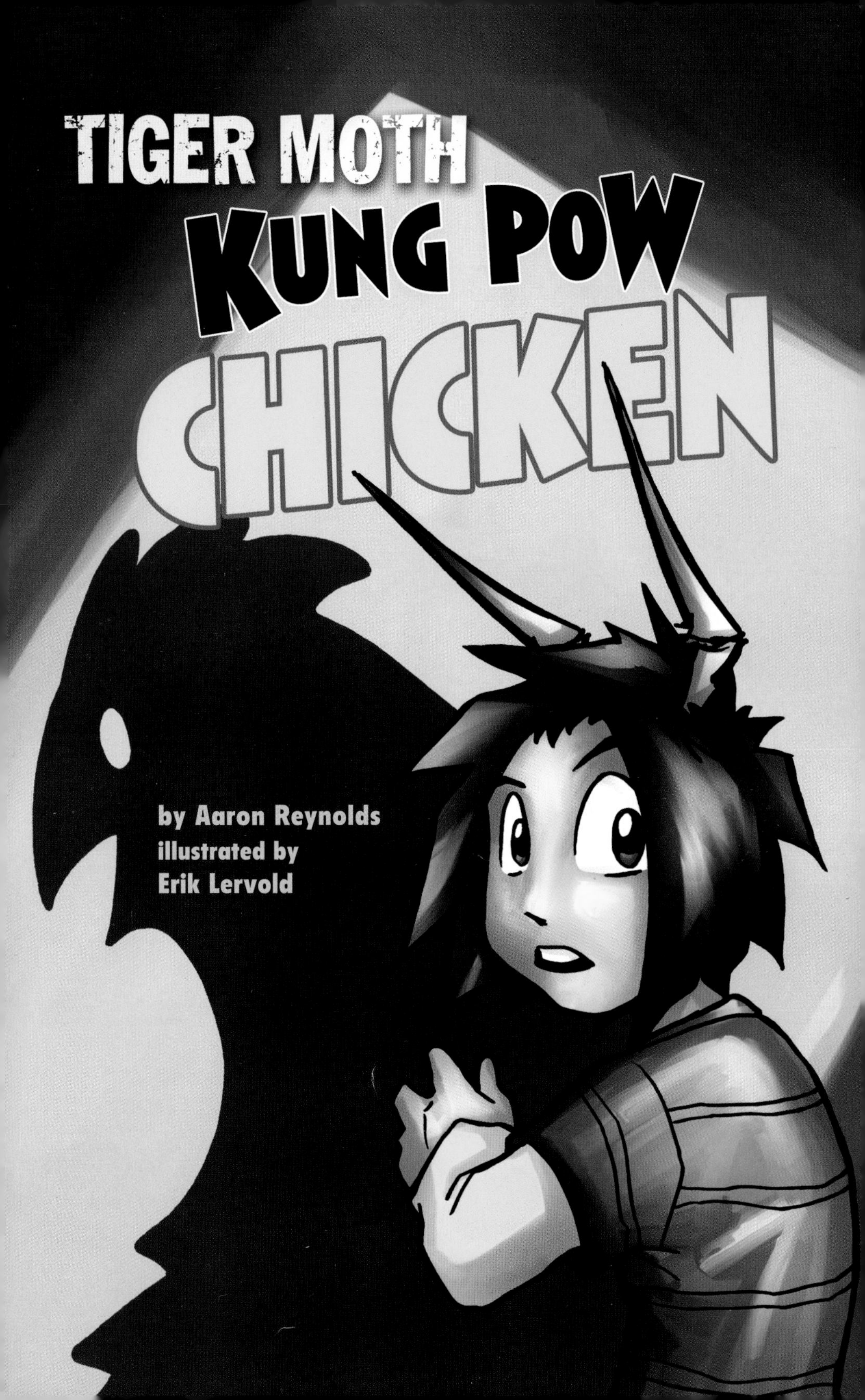
TIGER MOTH
KUNG POW
CHICKEN
by Aaron Reynolds
illustrated by
Erik Lervold

CAST OF CHARACTERS

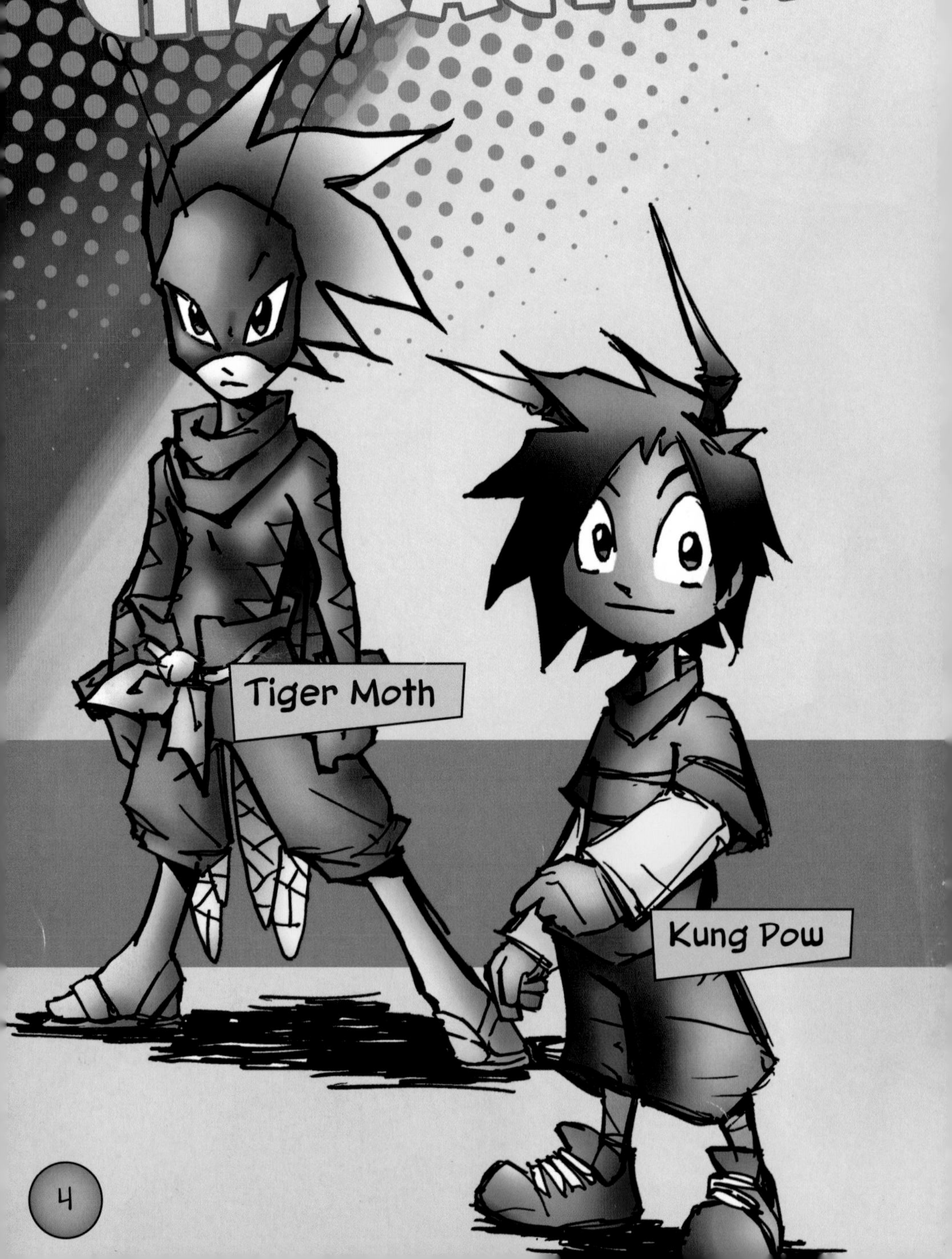
Tiger Moth
Kung Pow

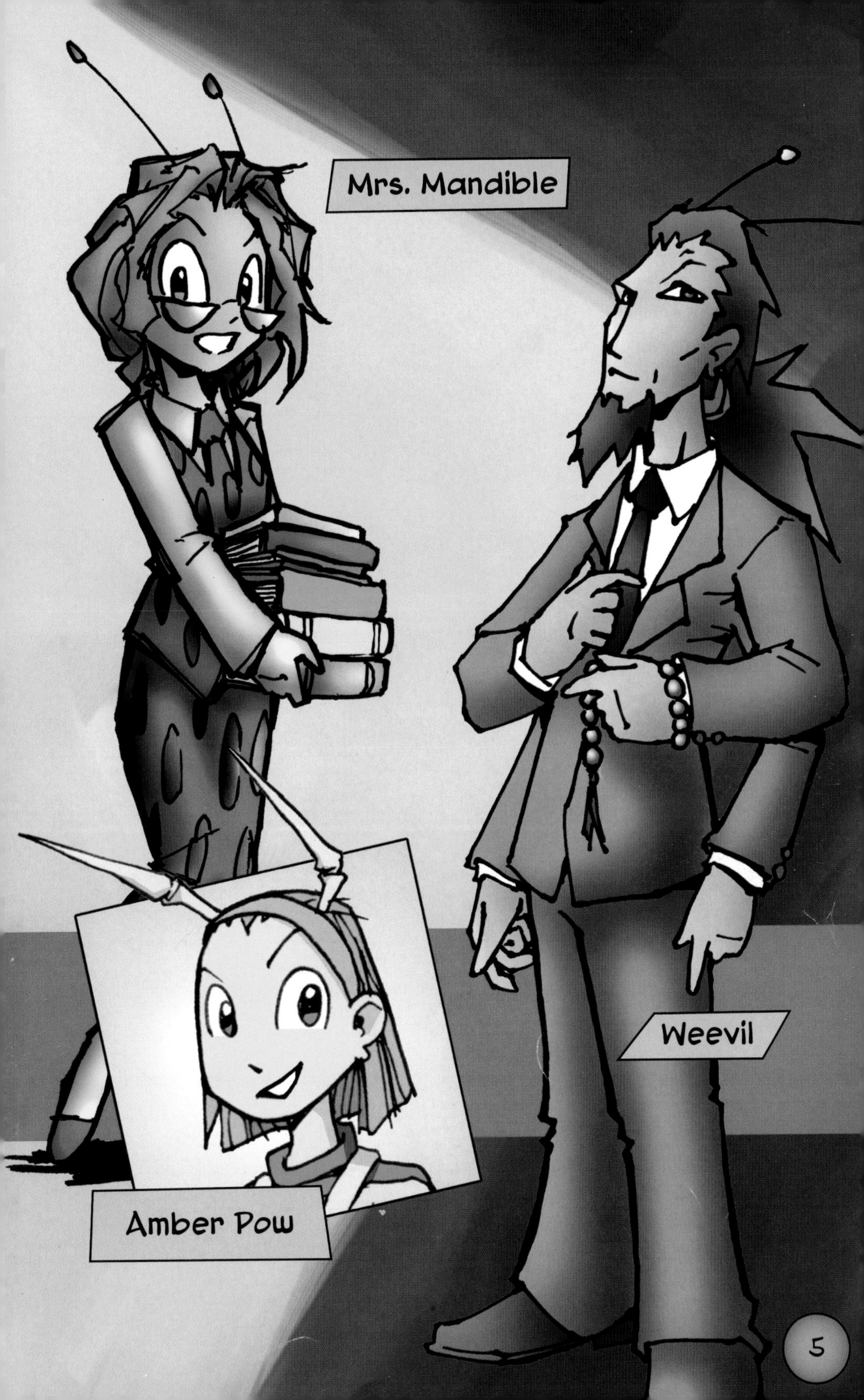
Mrs. Mandible
Weevil
Amber Pow

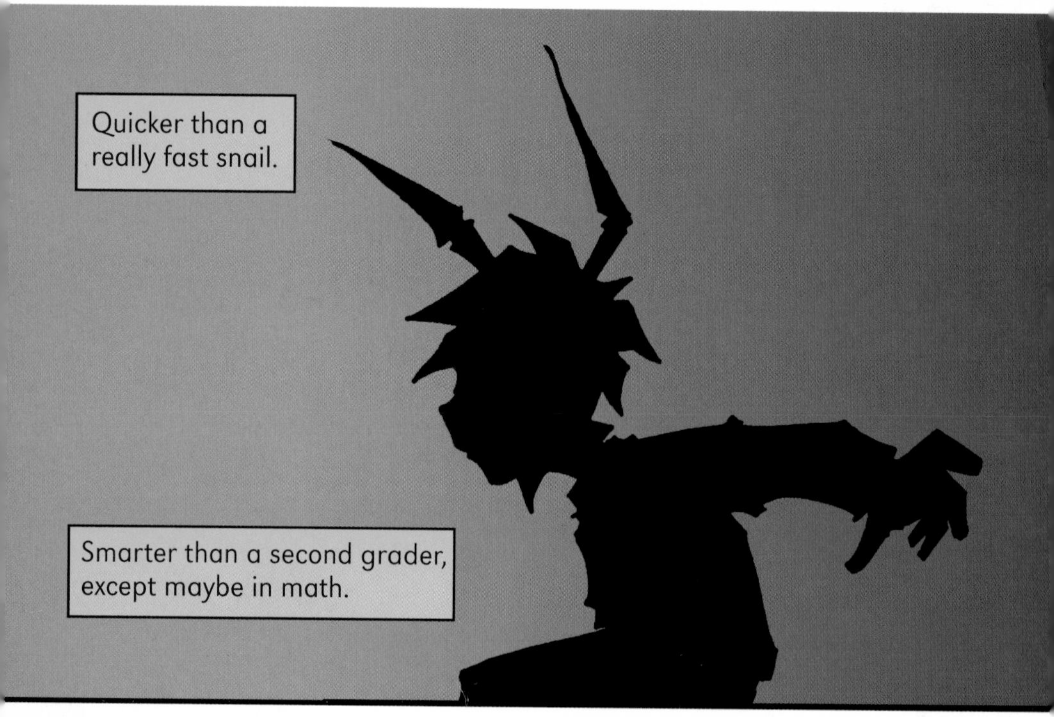
Quicker than a really fast snail.
Smarter than a second grader, except maybe in math.

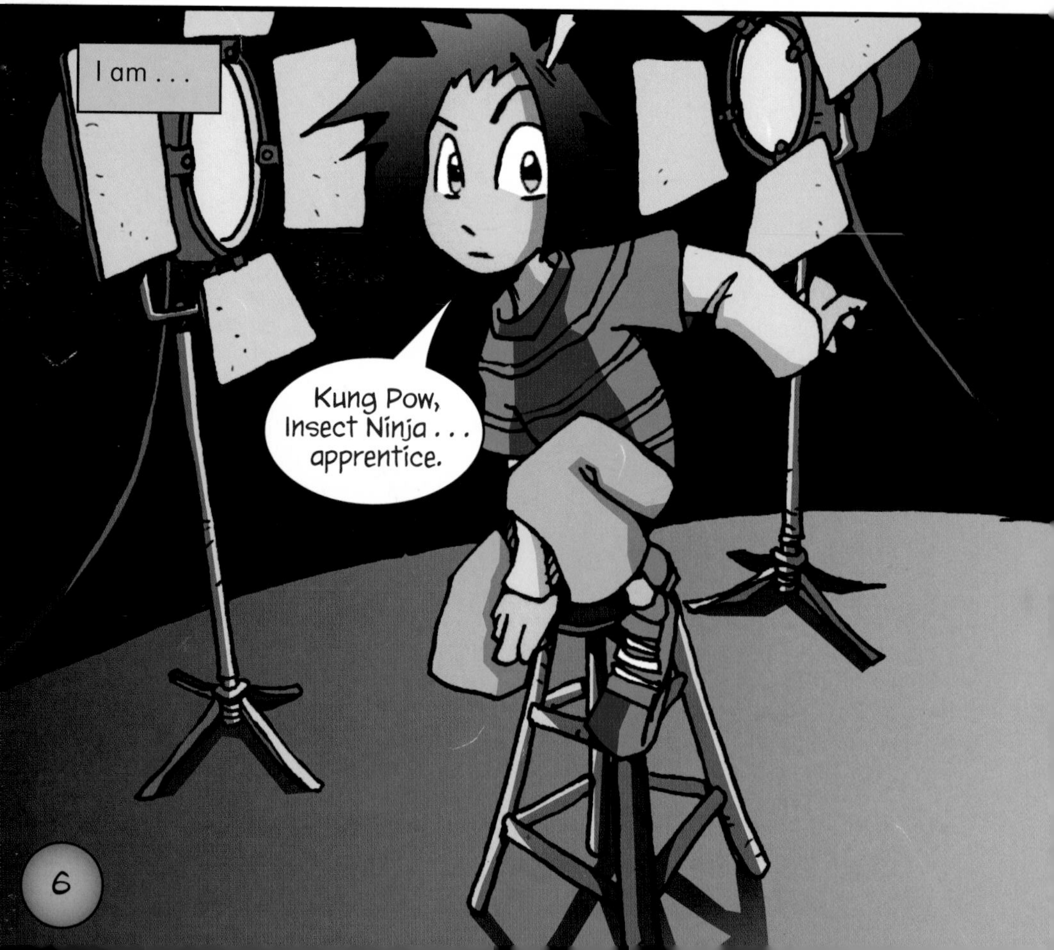
I am . . .
Kung Pow, Insect Ninja . . . apprentice.

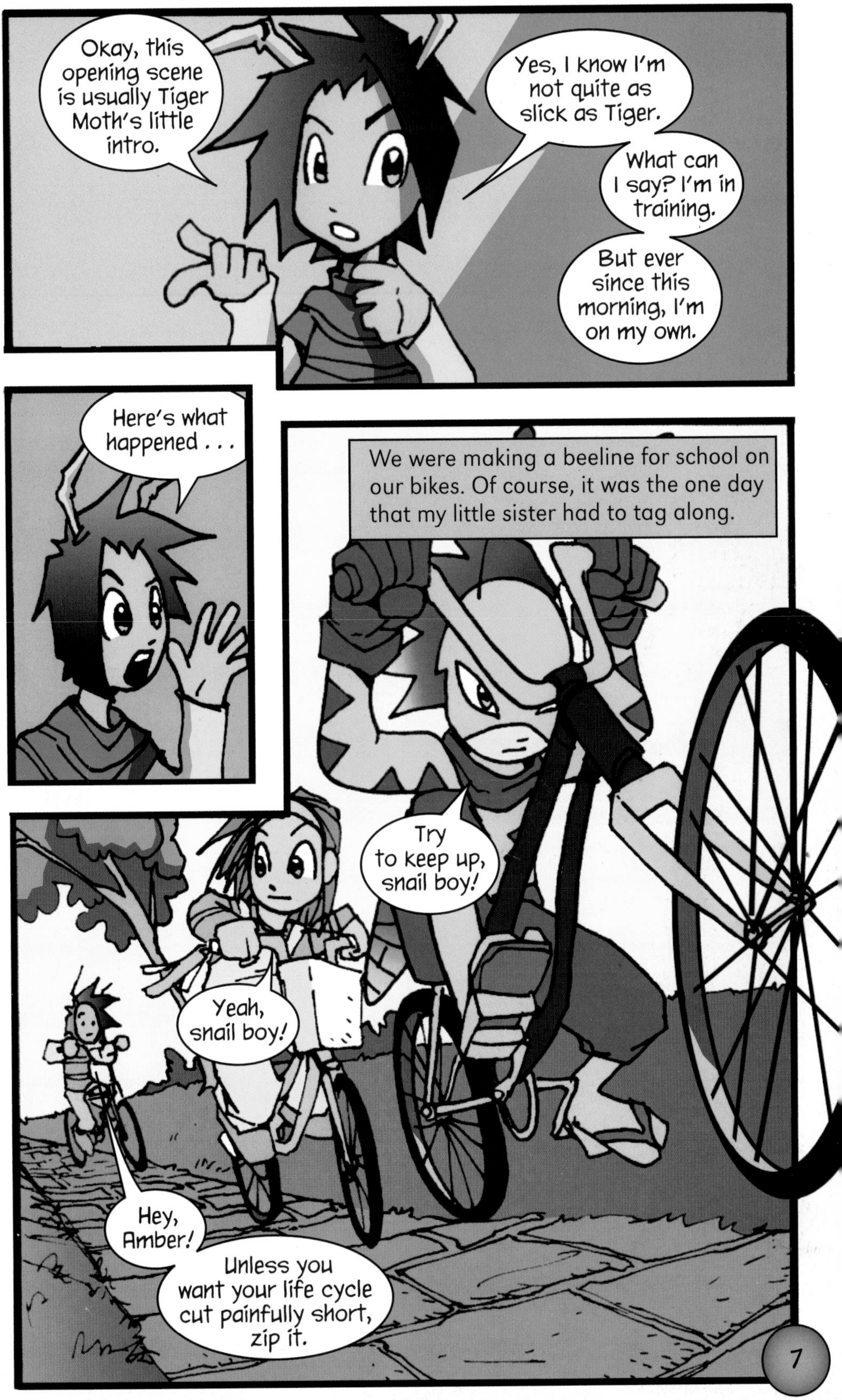
Okay, this opening scene is usually Tiger Moth's little intro.
Yes, I know I'm not quite as slick as Tiger.
What can I say? I'm in training.
But ever since this morning, I'm on my own.
Here's what happened . . .
We were making a beeline for school on our bikes. Of course, it was the one day that my little sister had to tag along.
Try to keep up, snail boy!
Yeah, snail boy!
Hey, Amber!
Unless you want your life cycle cut painfully short, zip it.

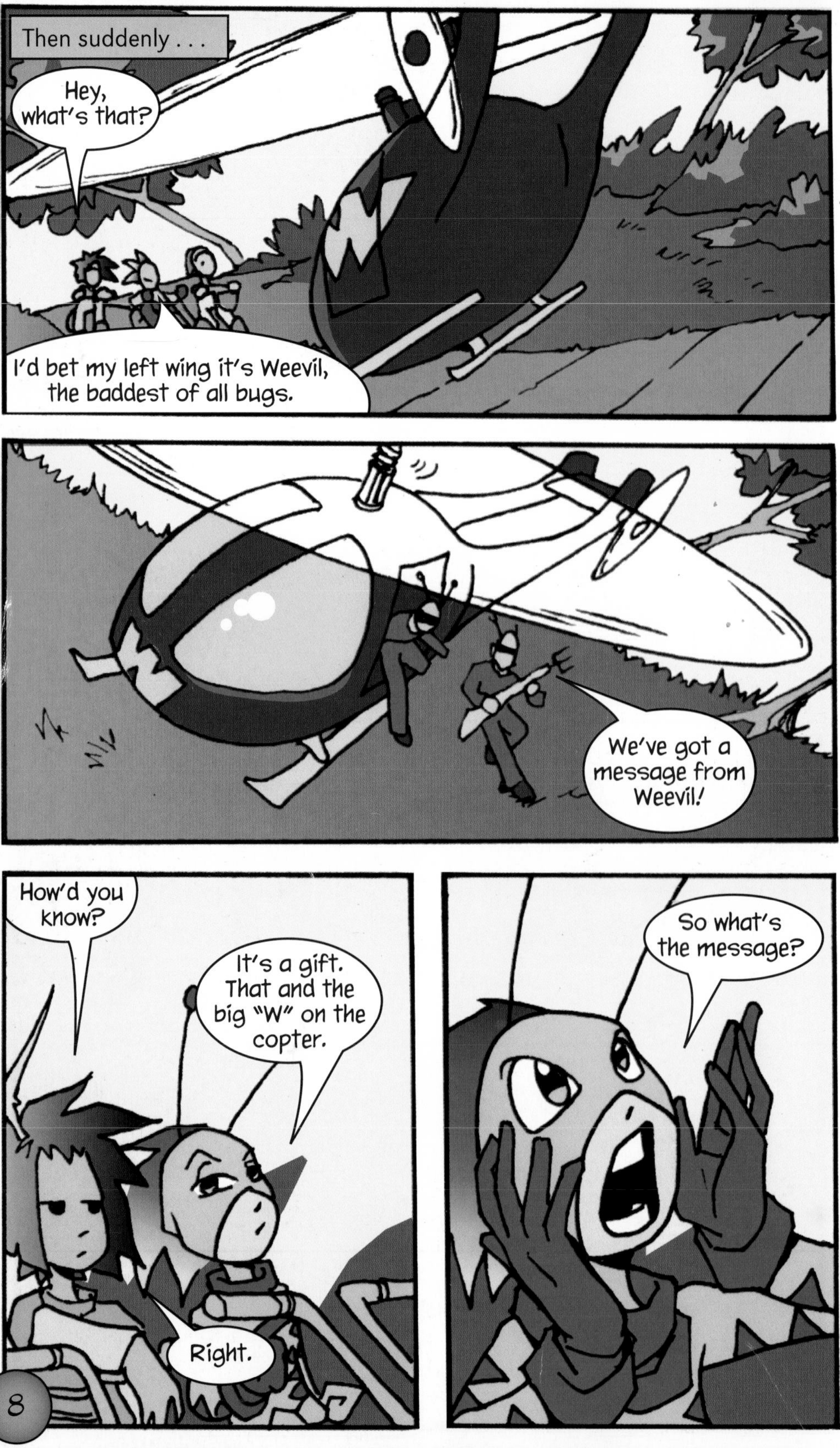
Then suddenly . . .
Hey, what's that?
I'd bet my left wing it's Weevil, the baddest of all bugs.
We've got a message from Weevil!
How'd you know?
It's a gift. That and the big "W" on the copter.
Right.
So what's the message?

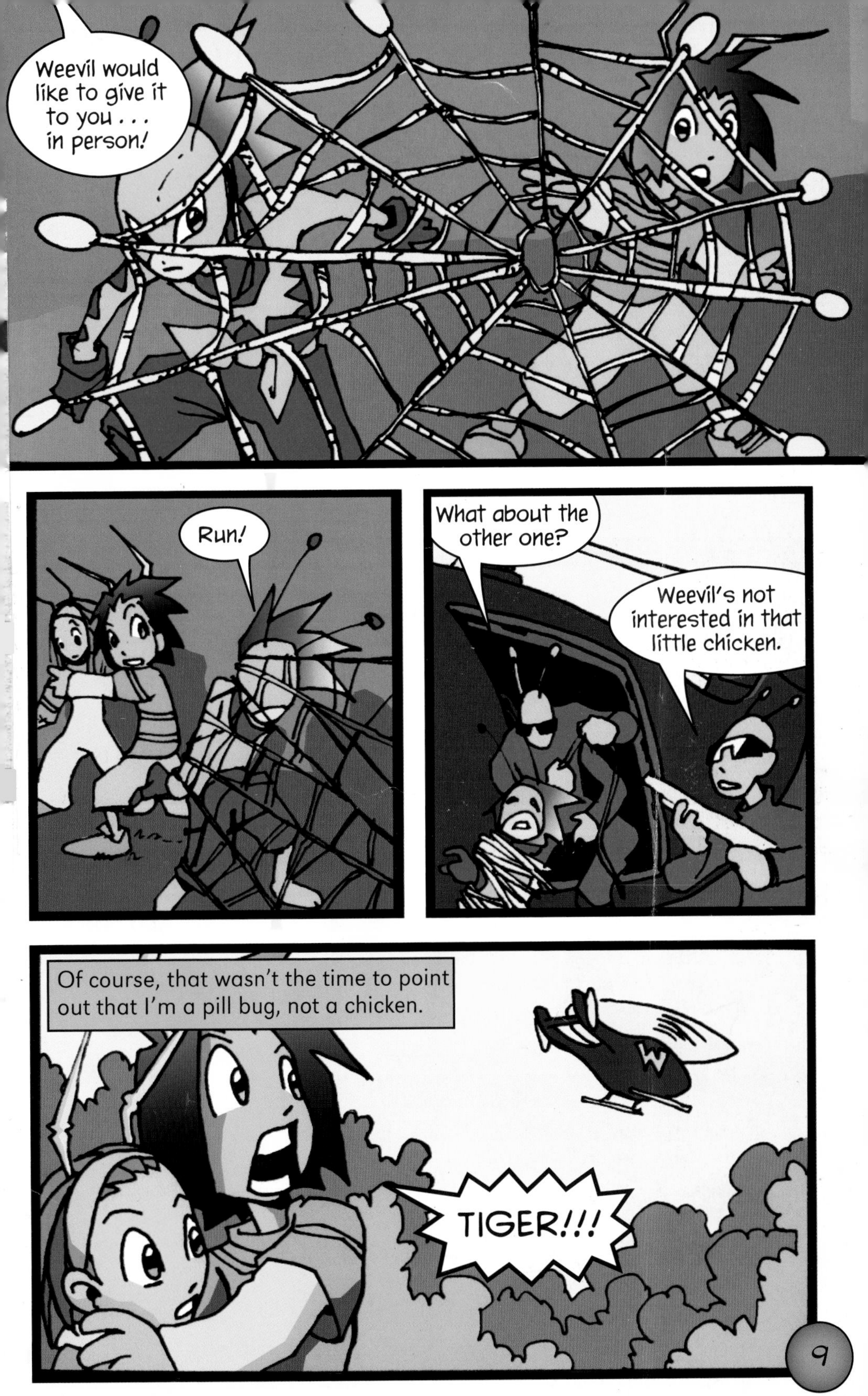
Weevil would like to give it to you . . . in person!
Run!
What about the other one?
Weevil's not interested in that little chicken.
Of course, that wasn't the time to point out that I'm a pill bug, not a chicken.
TIGER!!!

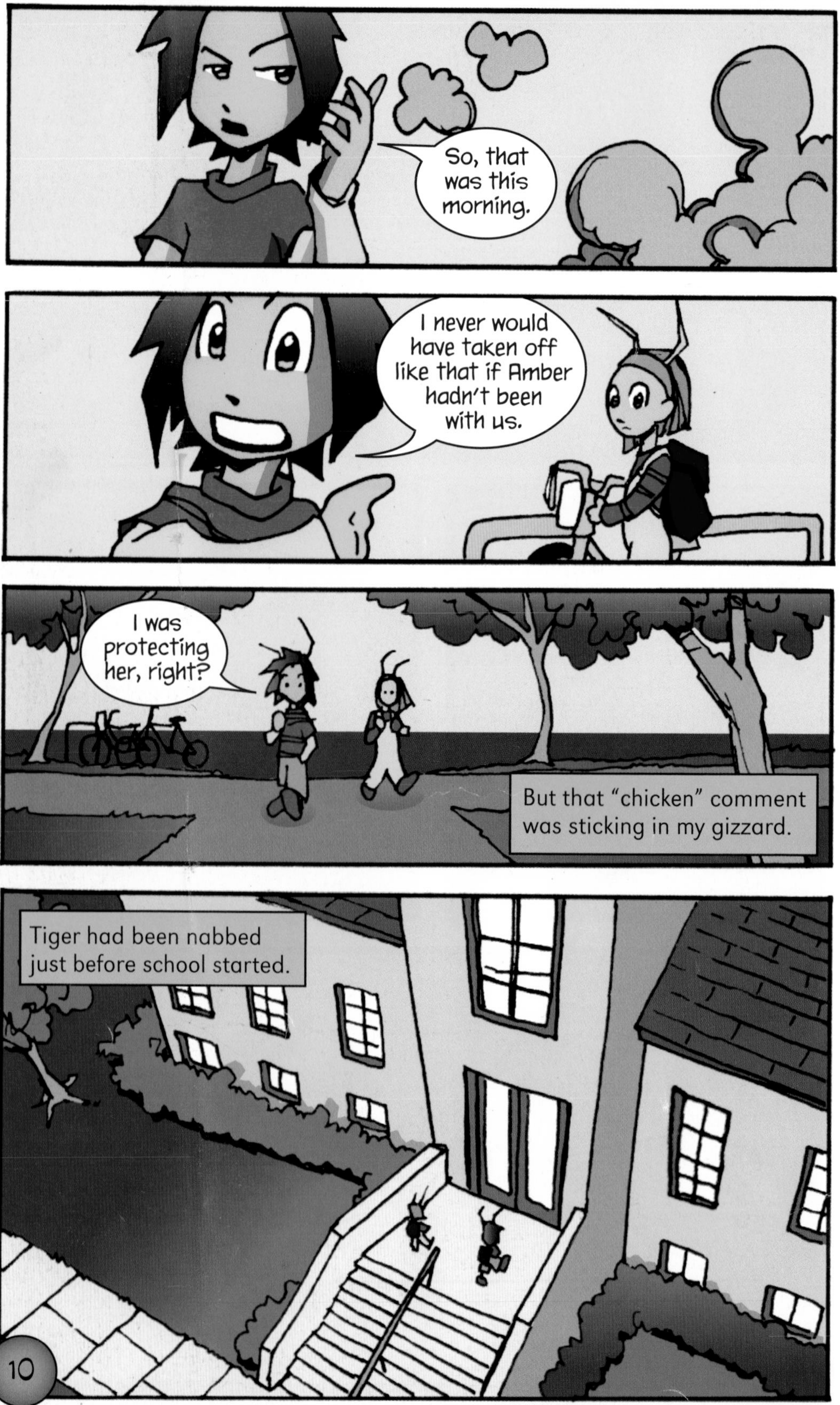
So, that was this morning.
I never would have taken off like that if Amber hadn't been with us.
I was protecting her, right?
But that "chicken" comment was sticking in my gizzard.
Tiger had been nabbed just before school started.

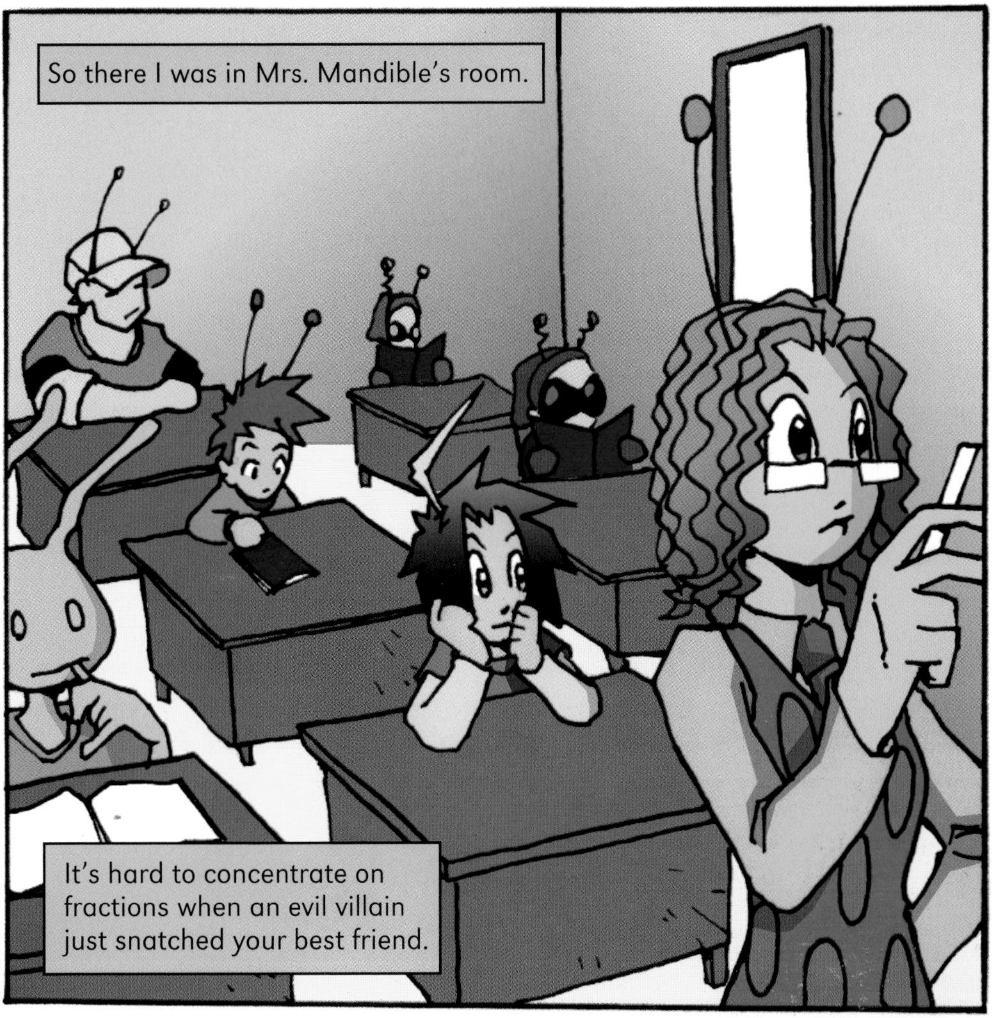
So there I was in Mrs. Mandible's room.
It's hard to concentrate on fractions when an evil villain just snatched your best friend.

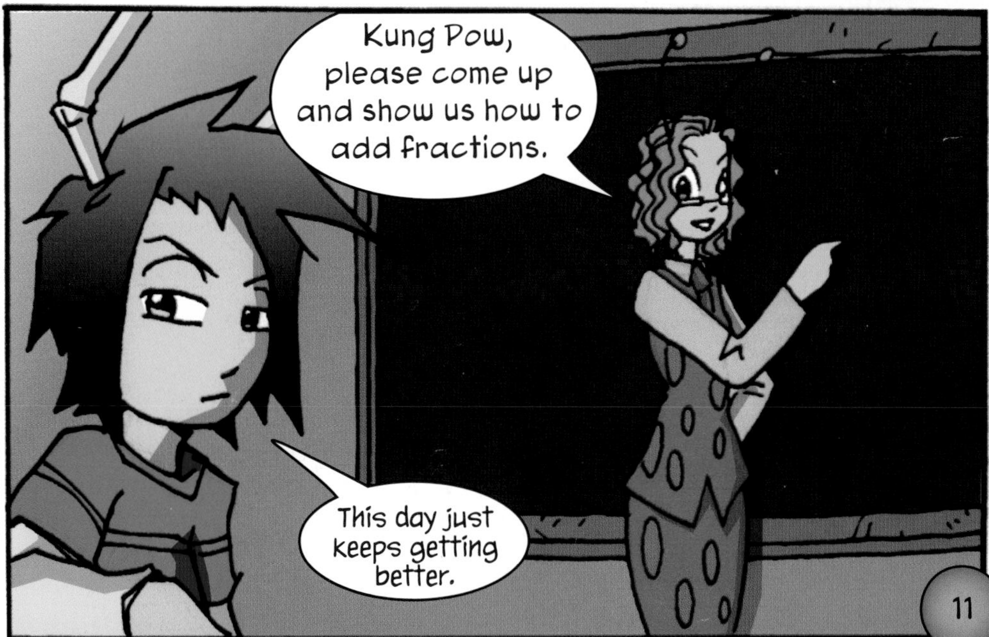
Kung Pow, please come up and show us how to add fractions.
This day just keeps getting better.

Tiger's at the mercy of that psycho, Weevil.

I'm standing here in class doing nothing about it.

But what can I do? I'm just an apprentice.

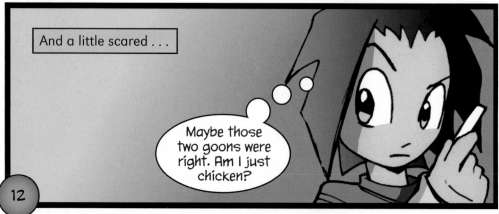

And a little scared . . .

Maybe those two goons were right. Am I just chicken?

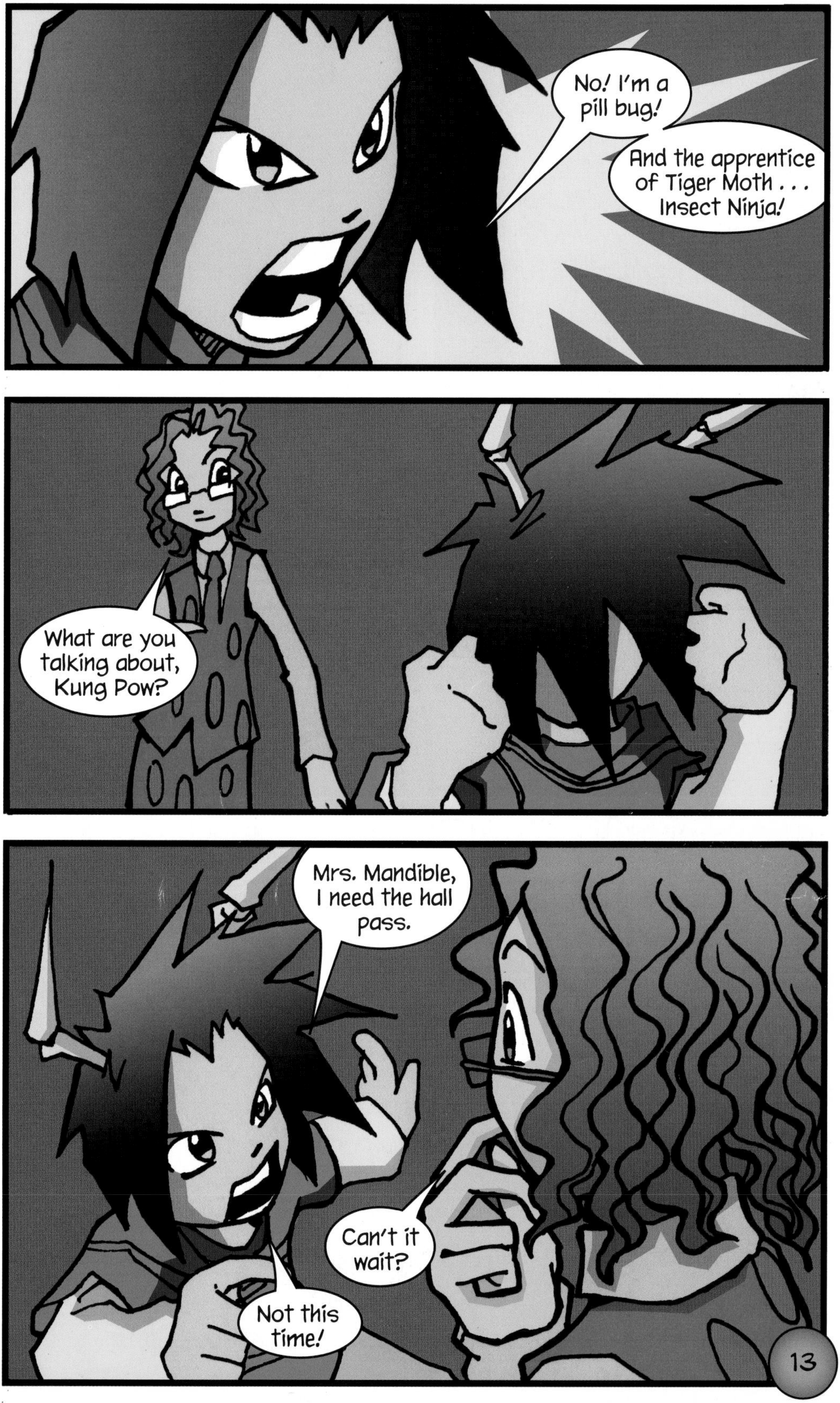
No! I'm a pill bug!
And the apprentice of Tiger Moth . . . Insect Ninja!
What are you talking about, Kung Pow?
Mrs. Mandible, I need the hall pass.
Can't it wait?
Not this time!

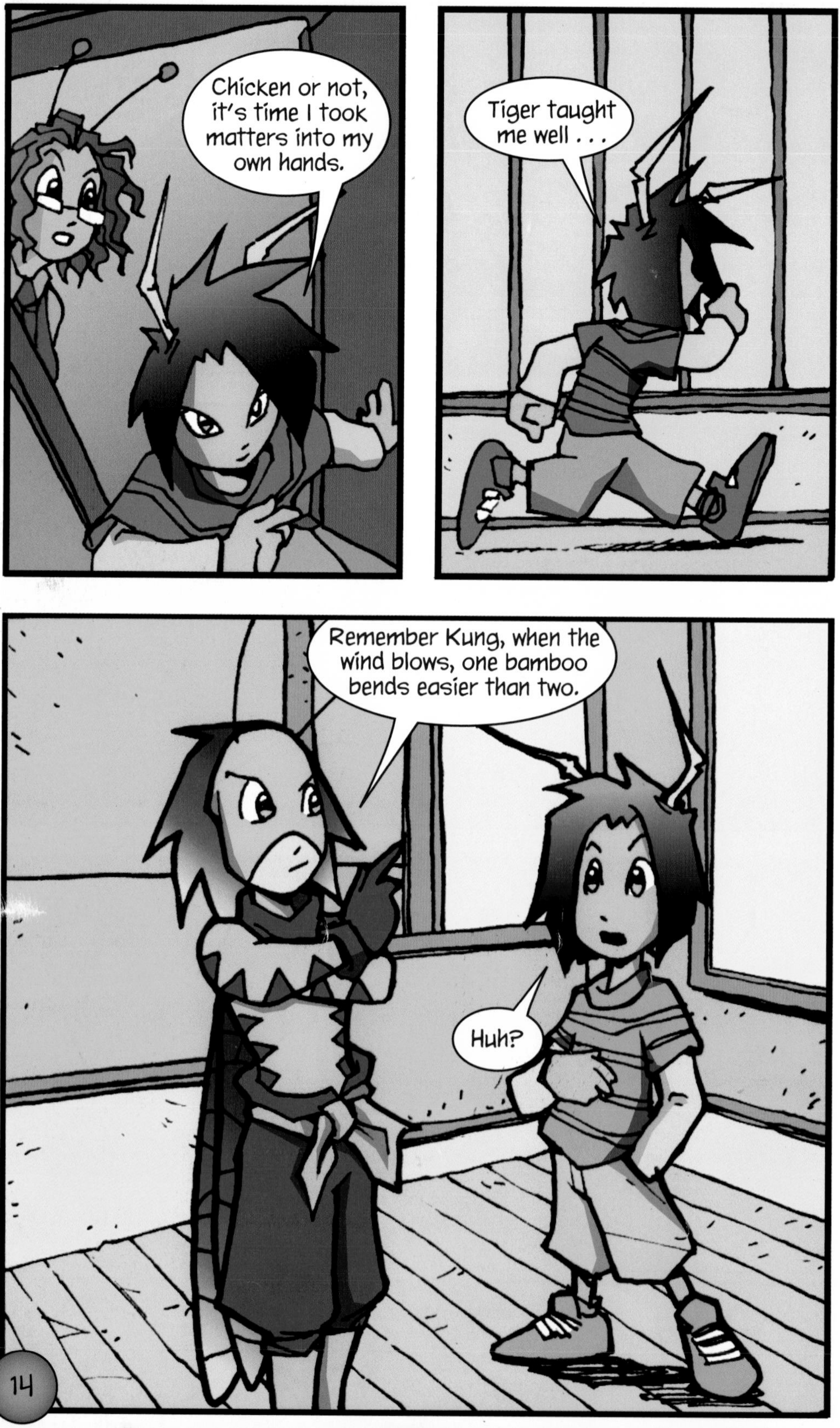
Chicken or not, it's time I took matters into my own hands.
Tiger taught me well . . .
Remember Kung, when the wind blows, one bamboo bends easier than two.
Huh?

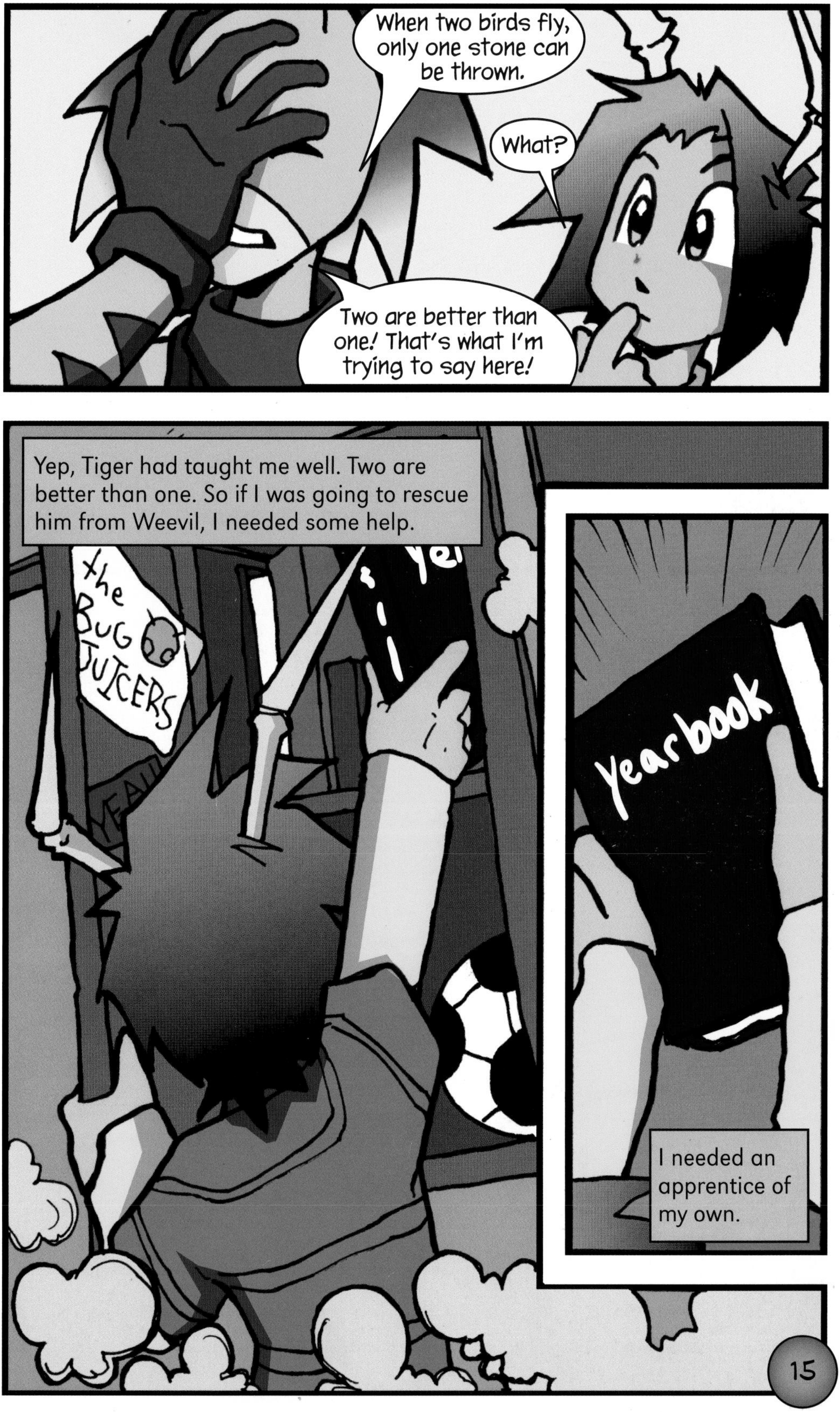
When two birds fly, only one stone can be thrown.
What?
Two are better than one! That's what I'm trying to say here!
Yep, Tiger had taught me well. Two are better than one. So if I was going to rescue him from Weevil, I needed some help.
the BUG JUICERS
Yearbook
I needed an apprentice of my own.

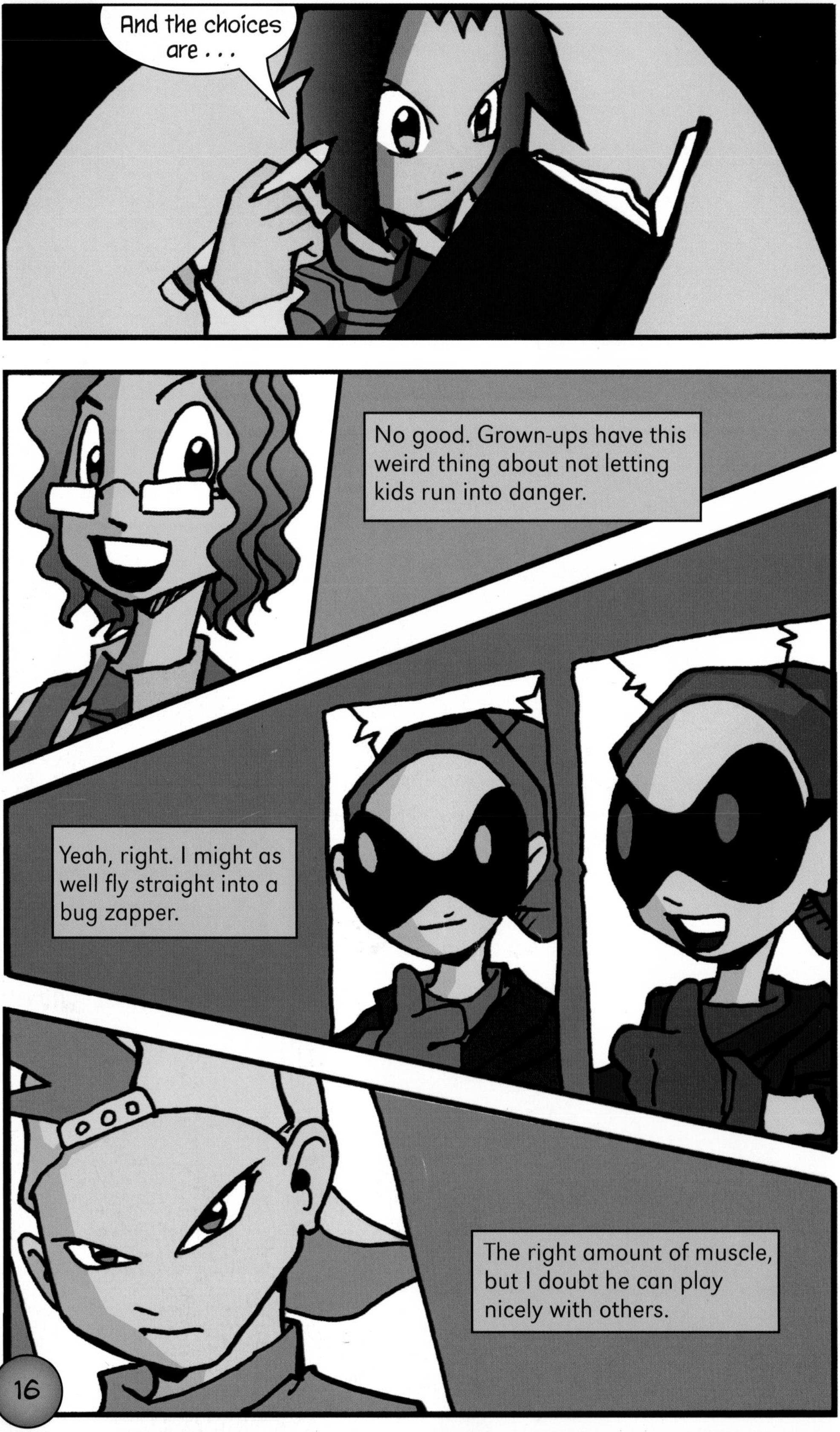
And the choices are . . .
No good. Grown-ups have this weird thing about not letting kids run into danger.
Yeah, right. I might as well fly straight into a bug zapper.
The right amount of muscle, but I doubt he can play nicely with others.

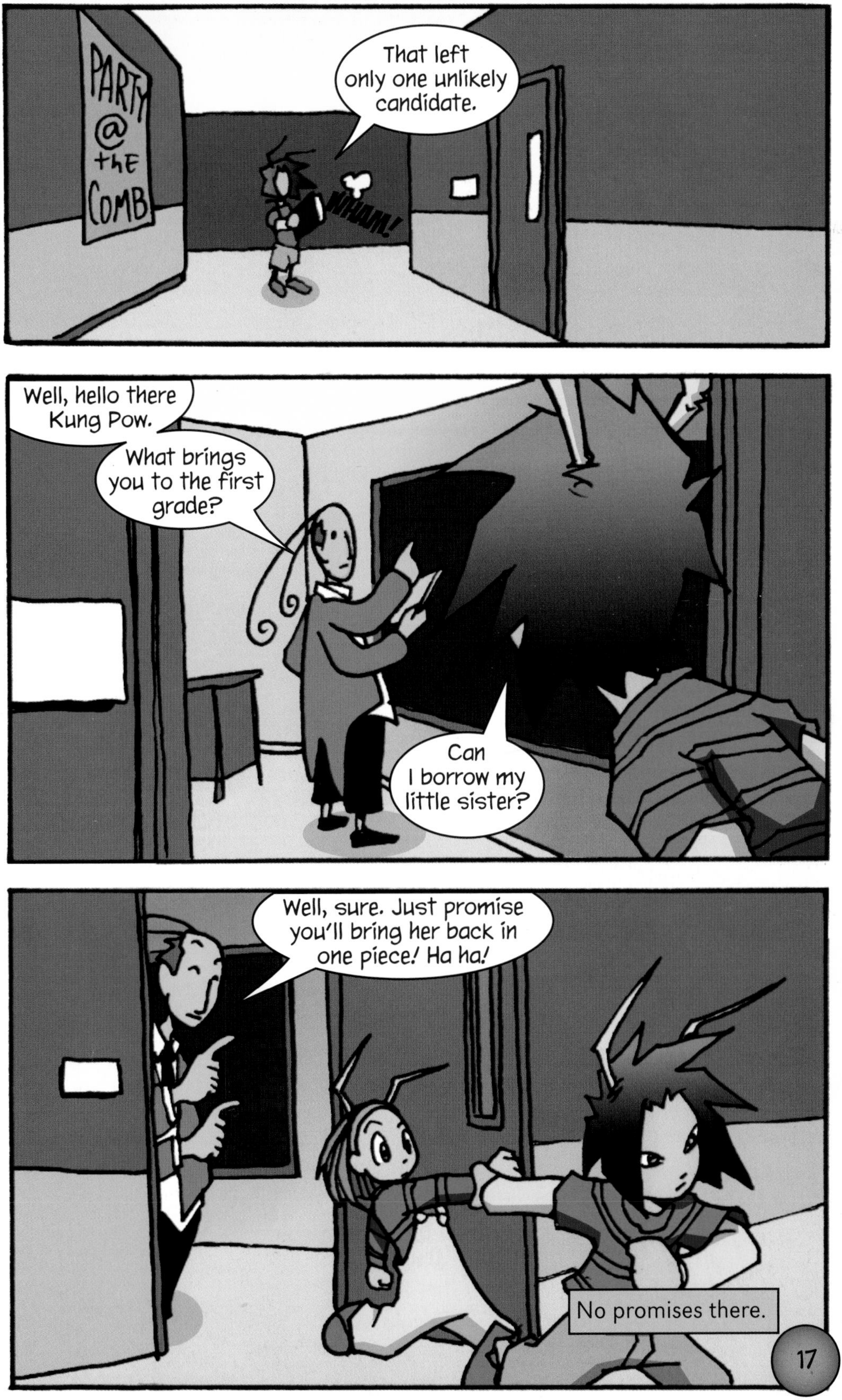
PARTY @ the COMB
That left only one unlikely candidate.
WHAM!
Well, hello there Kung Pow.
What brings you to the first grade?
Can I borrow my little sister?
Well, sure. Just promise you'll bring her back in one piece! Ha ha!
No promises there.

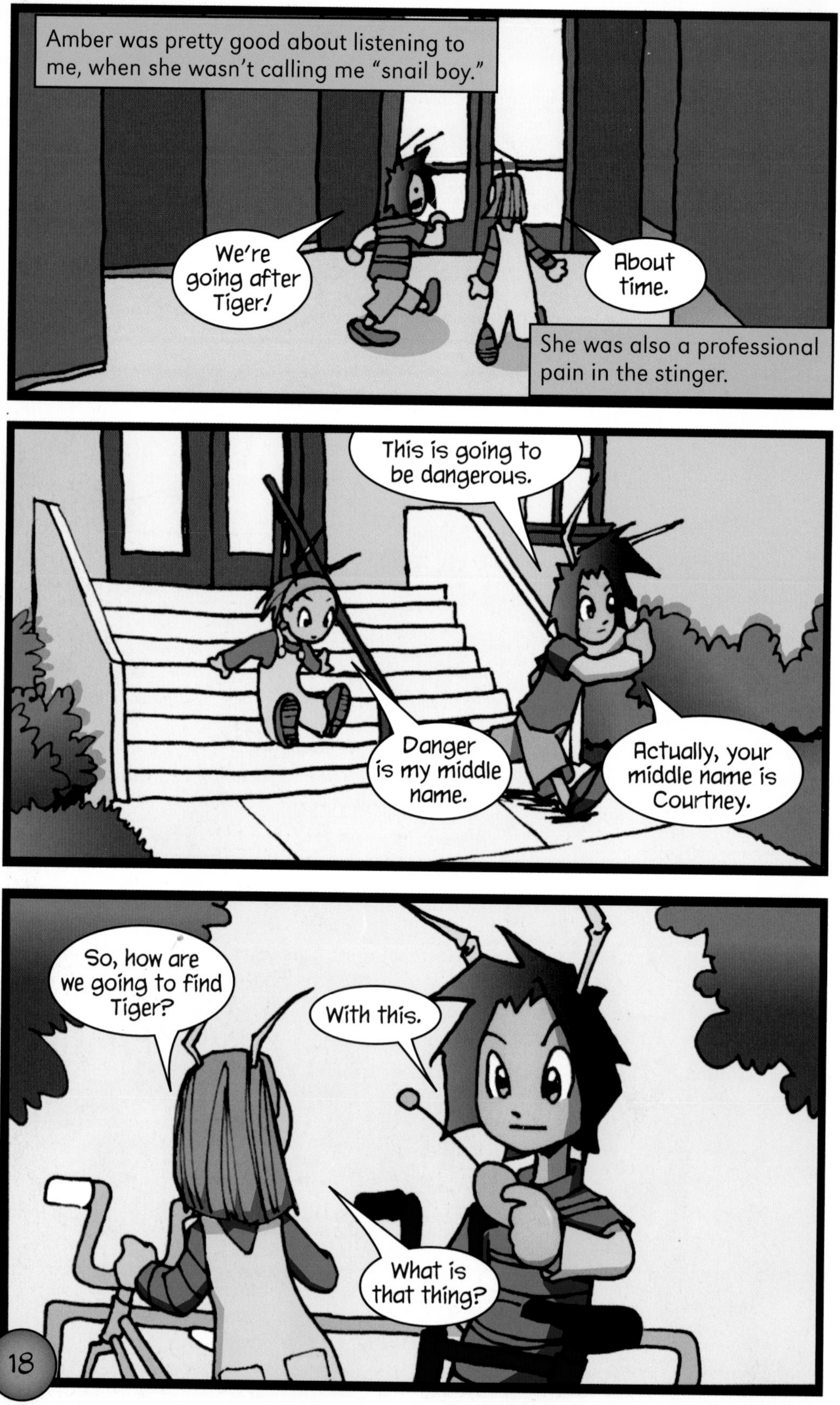
Amber was pretty good about listening to me, when she wasn't calling me "snail boy."
We're going after Tiger!
About time.
She was also a professional pain in the stinger.
This is going to be dangerous.
Danger is my middle name.
Actually, your middle name is Courtney.
So, how are we going to find Tiger?
With this.
What is that thing?

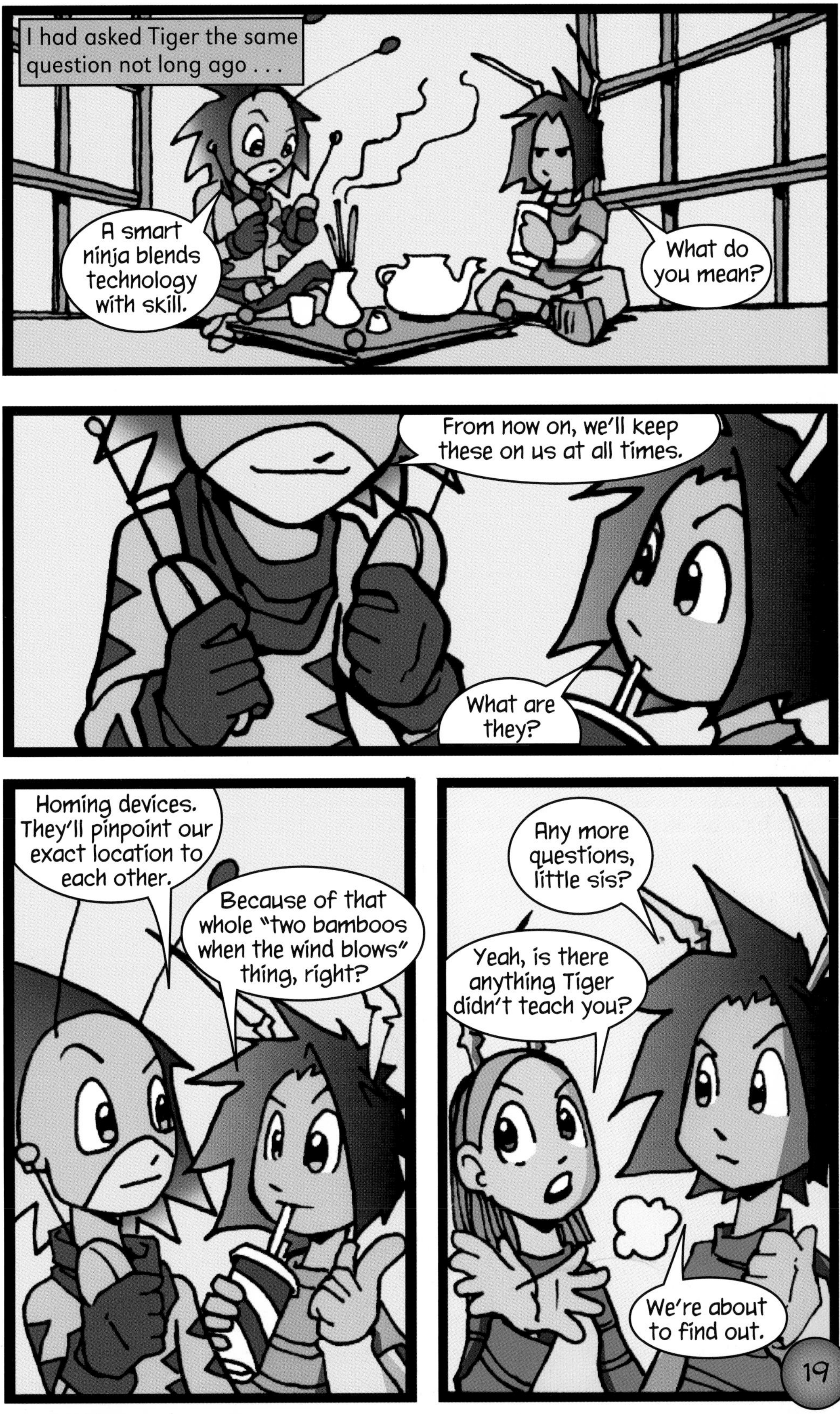
I had asked Tiger the same question not long ago . . .
A smart ninja blends technology with skill.
What do you mean?
From now on, we'll keep these on us at all times.
What are they?
Homing devices. They'll pinpoint our exact location to each other.
Because of that whole "two bamboos when the wind blows" thing, right?
Any more questions, little sis?
Yeah, is there anything Tiger didn't teach you?
We're about to find out.

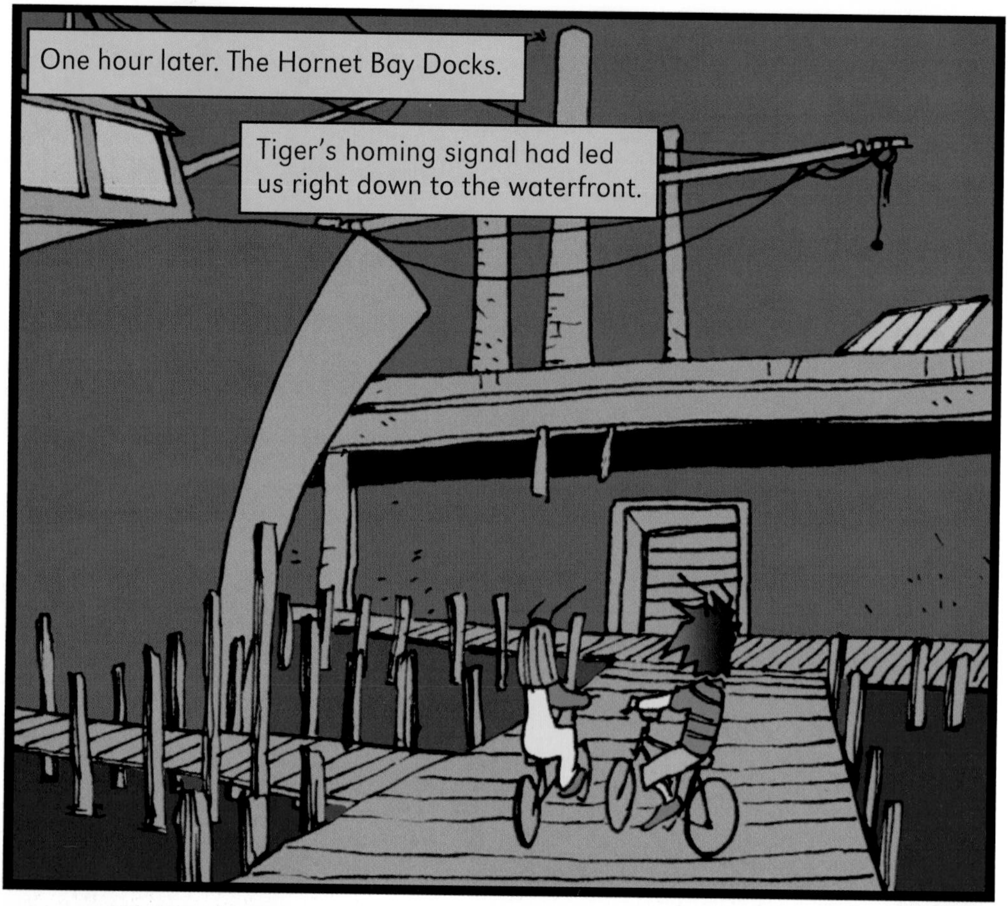
One hour later. The Hornet Bay Docks.
Tiger's homing signal had led us right down to the waterfront.

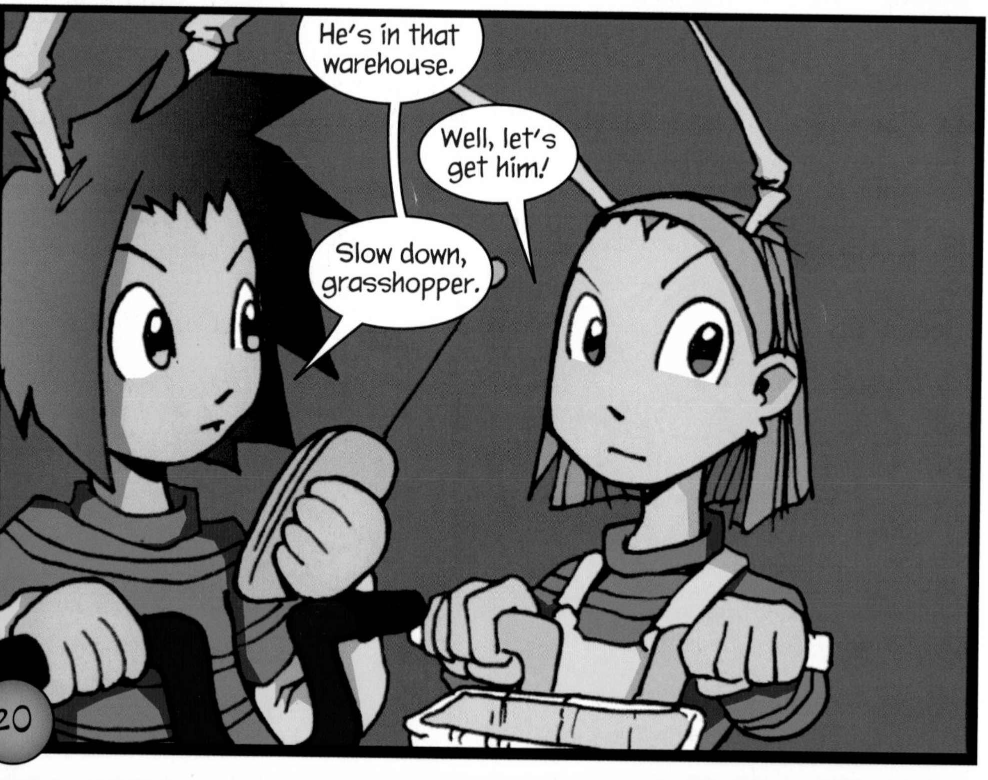
He's in that warehouse.
Well, let's get him!
Slow down, grasshopper.

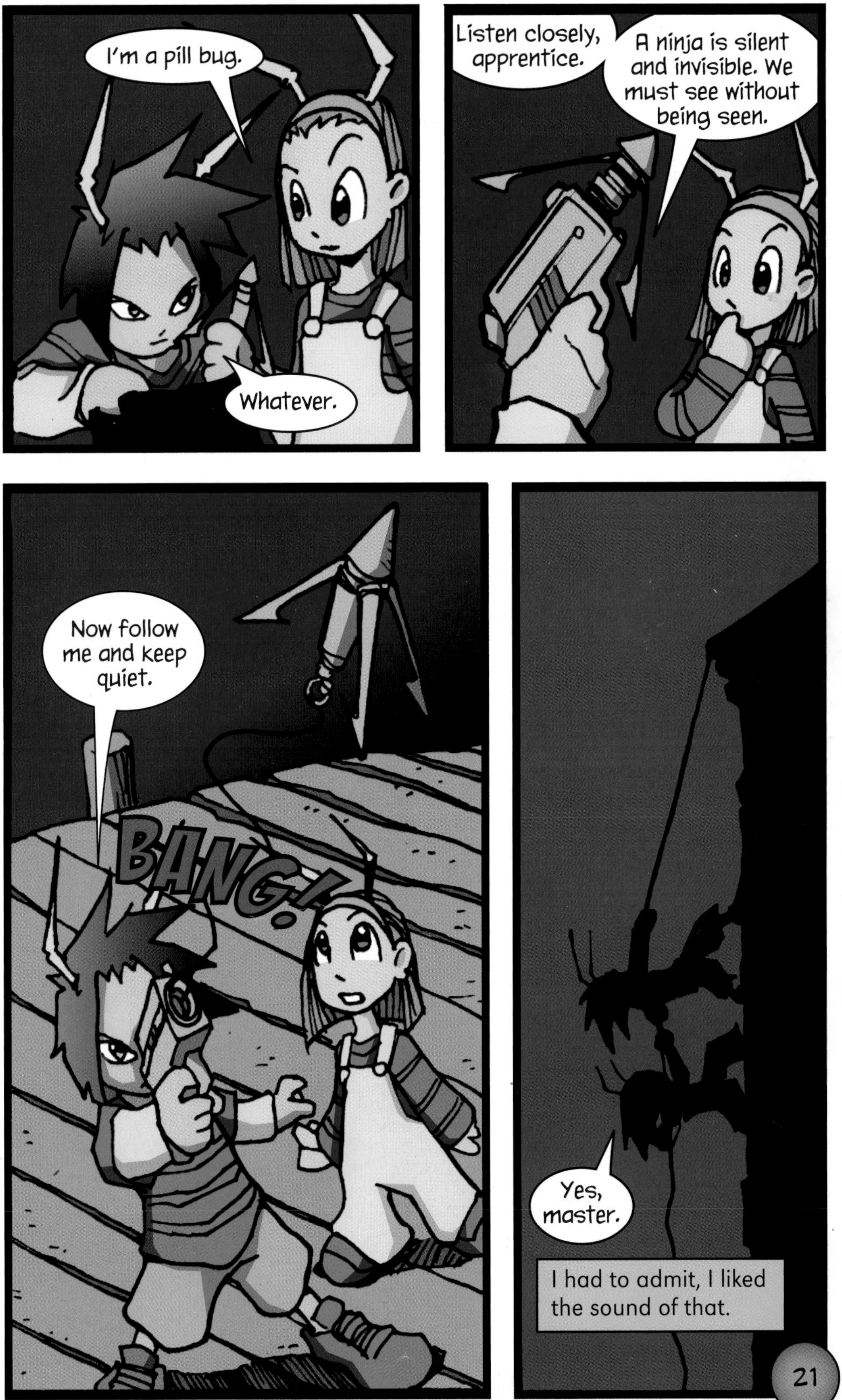
I'm a pill bug.
Whatever.
Listen closely, apprentice.
A ninja is silent and invisible. We must see without being seen.
Now follow me and keep quiet.
BANG!
Yes, master.
I had to admit, I liked the sound of that.

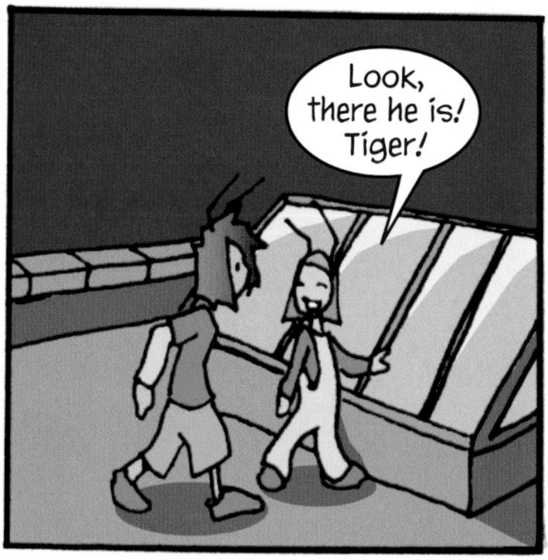
Look, there he is! Tiger!

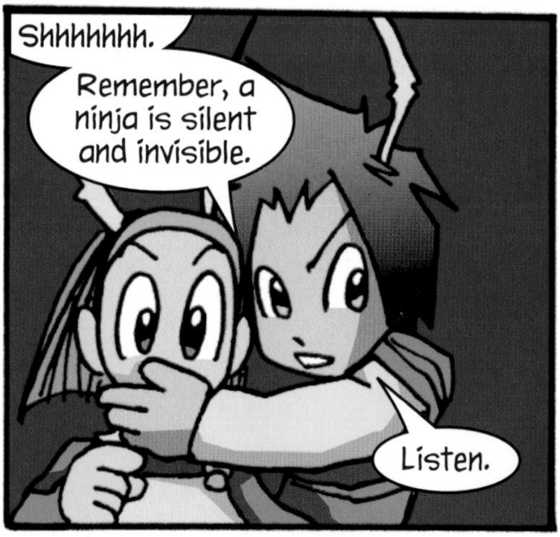
Shhhhhhh.
Remember, a ninja is silent and invisible.
Listen.

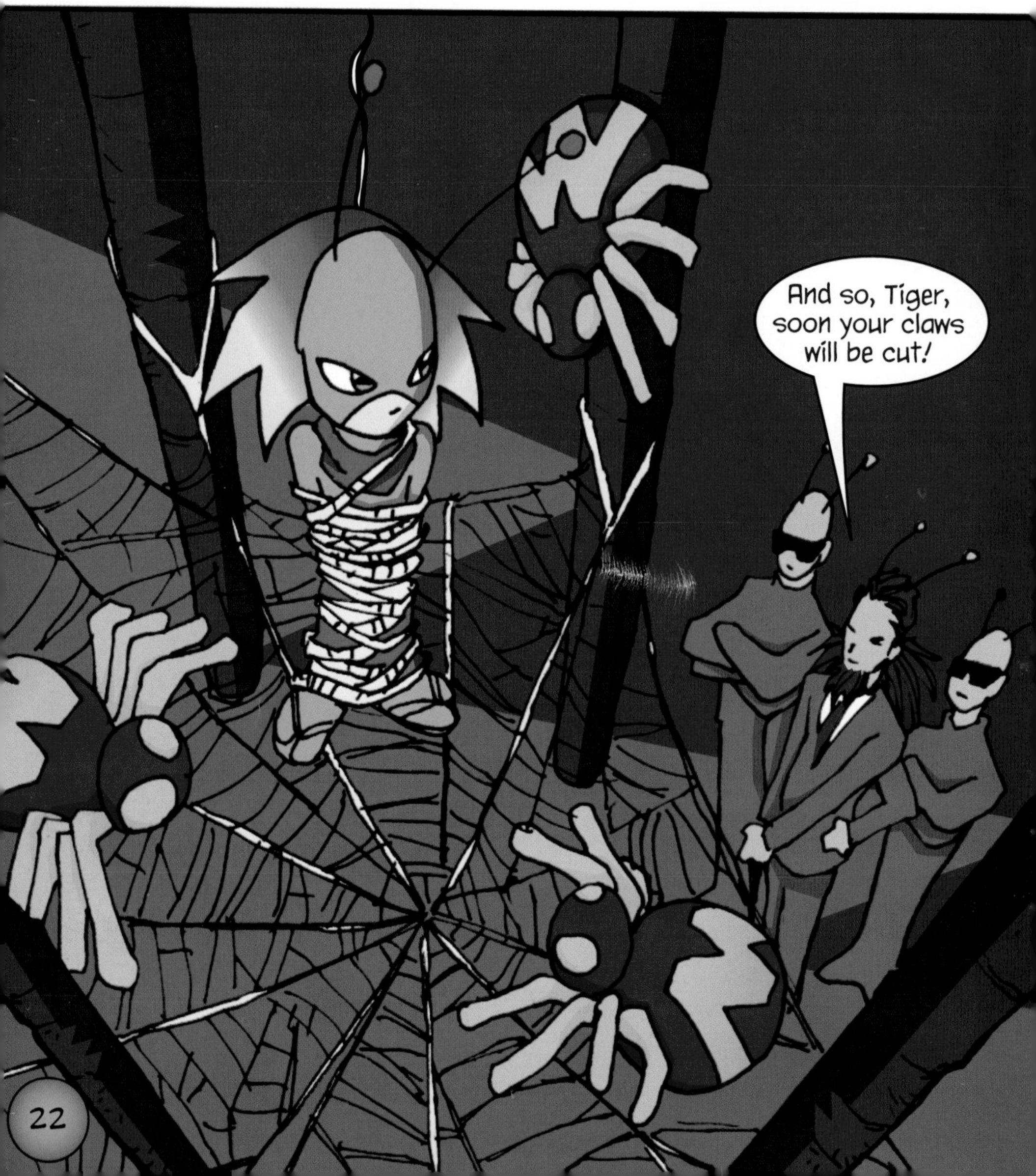
And so, Tiger, soon your claws will be cut!

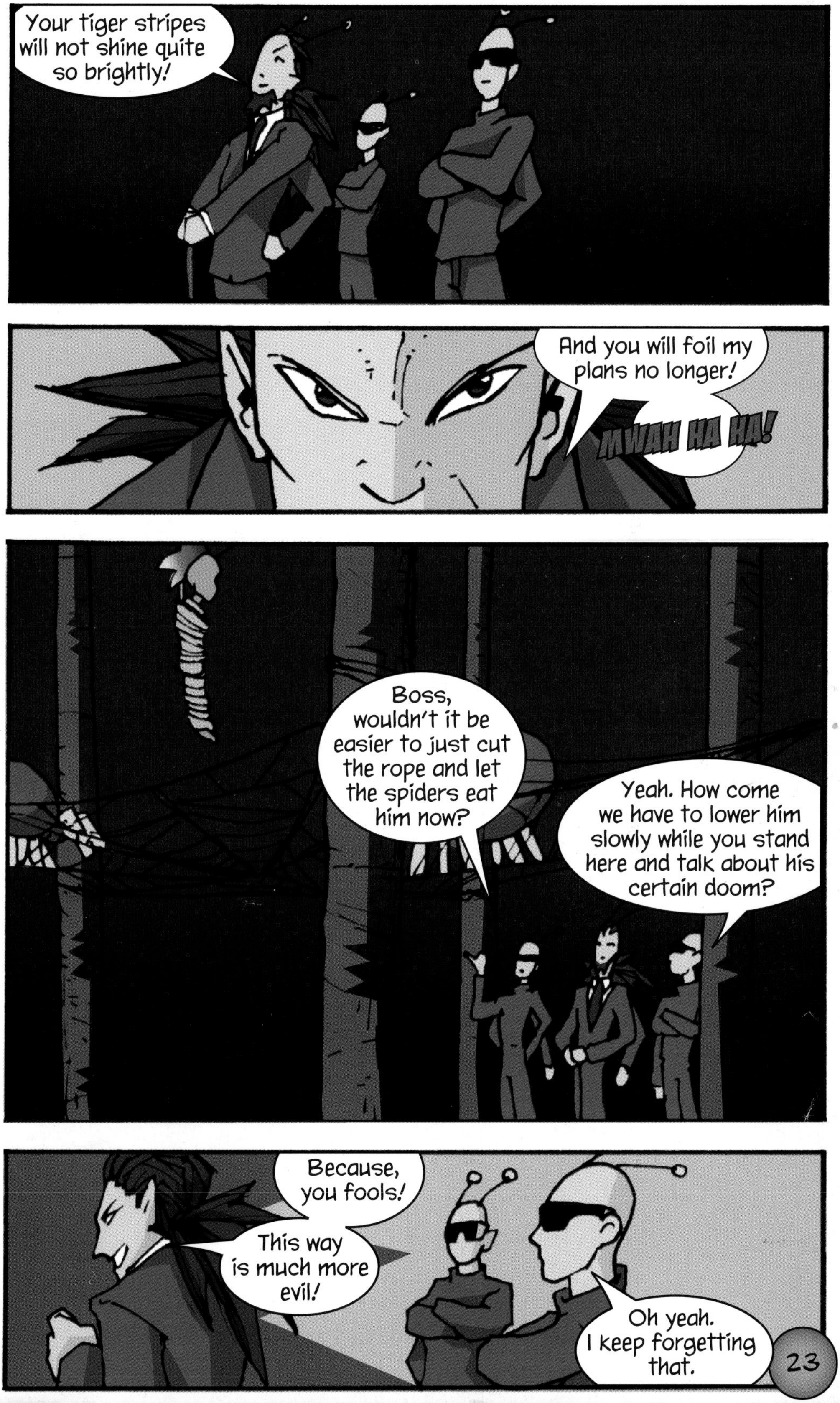
Your tiger stripes will not shine quite so brightly!
And you will foil my plans no longer!
MWAH HA HA!
Boss, wouldn't it be easier to just cut the rope and let the spiders eat him now?
Yeah. How come we have to lower him slowly while you stand here and talk about his certain doom?
Because, you fools!
This way is much more evil!
Oh yeah. I keep forgetting that.

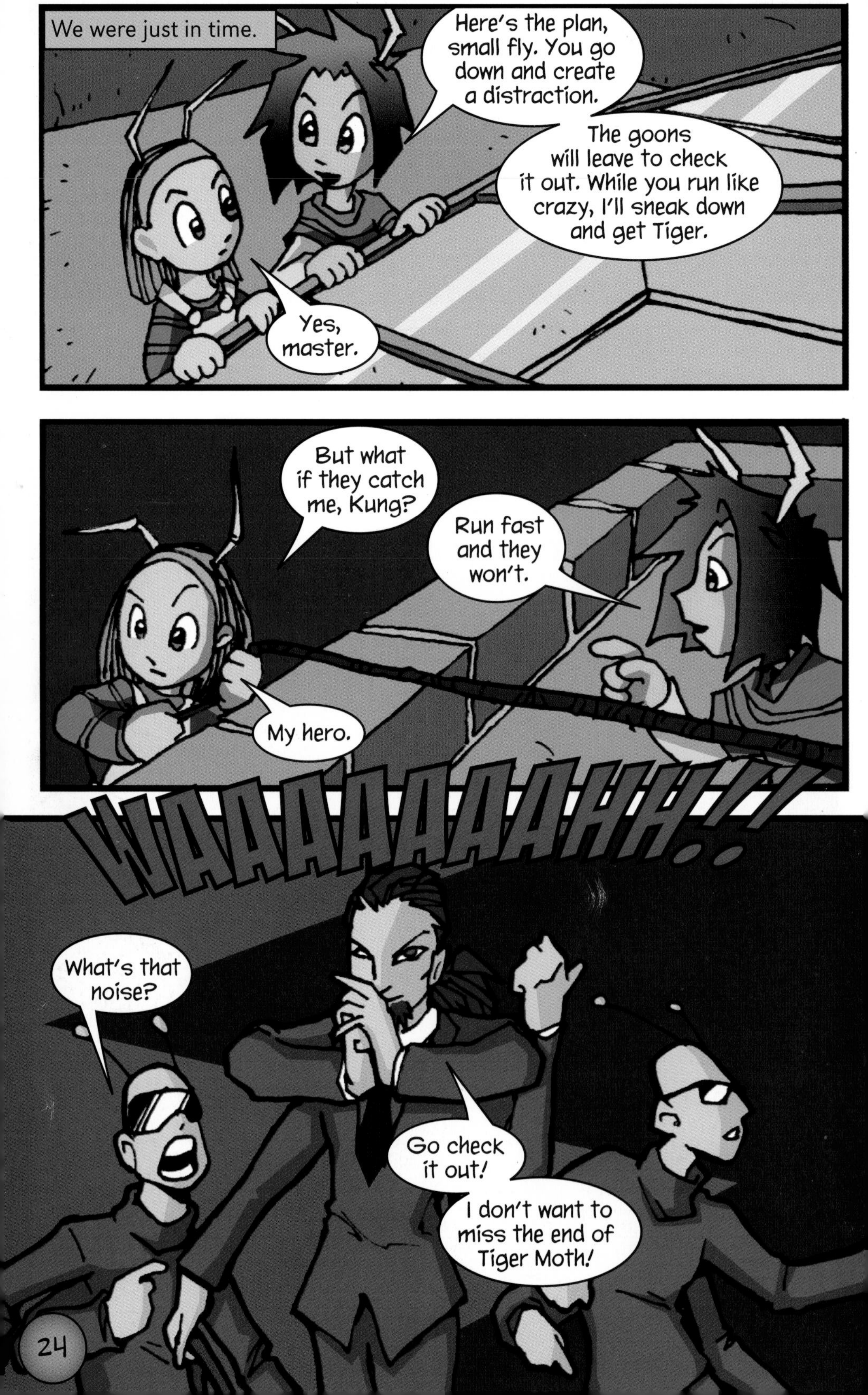
We were just in time.
Here's the plan, small fly. You go down and create a distraction.
The goons will leave to check it out. While you run like crazy, I'll sneak down and get Tiger.
Yes, master.
But what if they catch me, Kung?
Run fast and they won't.
My hero.
WAAAAAAAAHH!!!
What's that noise?
Go check it out!
I don't want to miss the end of Tiger Moth!

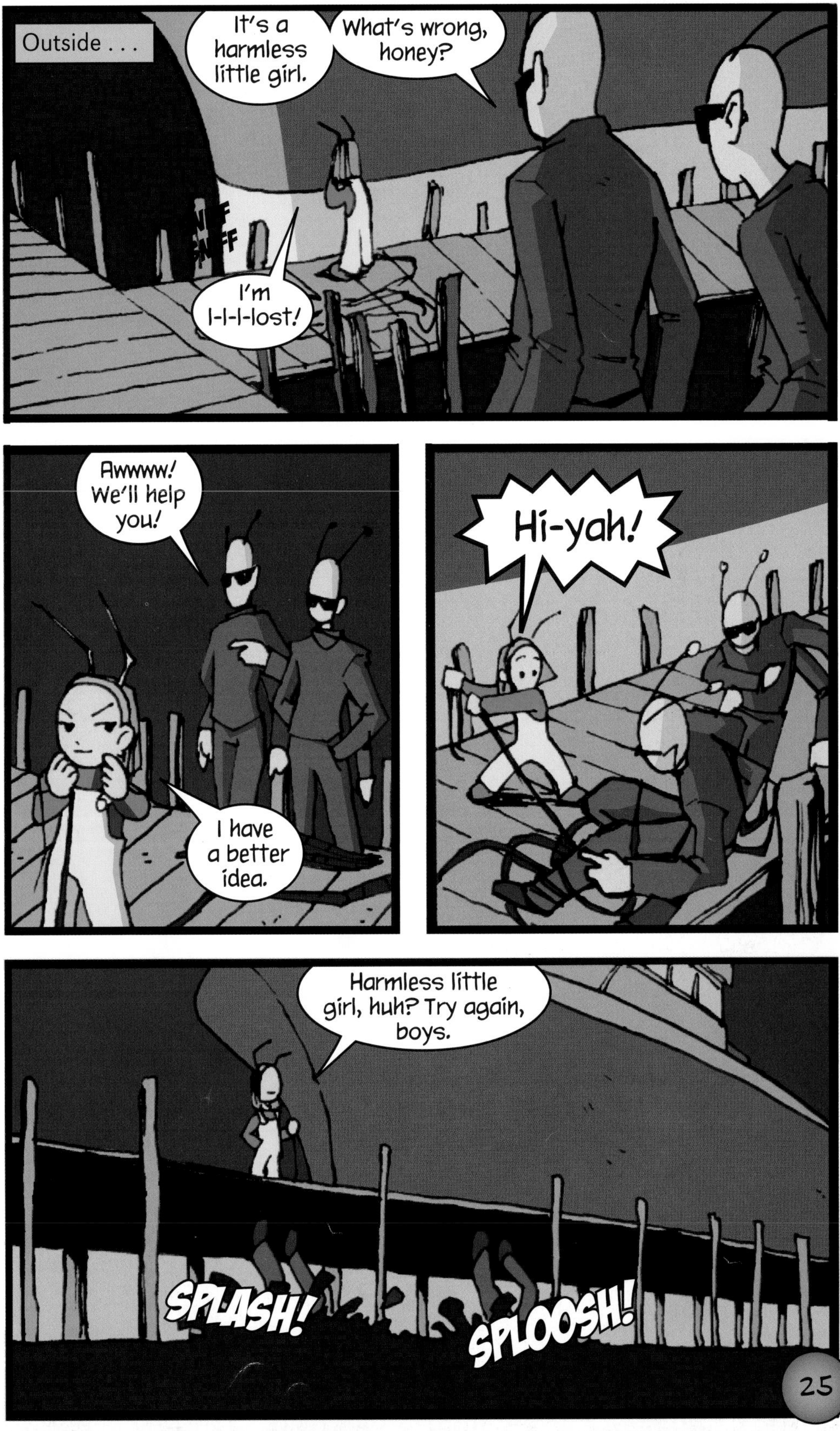
Outside . . .
It's a harmless little girl.
What's wrong, honey?
I'm l-l-l-lost!
Awwww! We'll help you!
I have a better idea.
Hi-yah!
Harmless little girl, huh? Try again, boys.
SPLASH!
SPLOOSH!

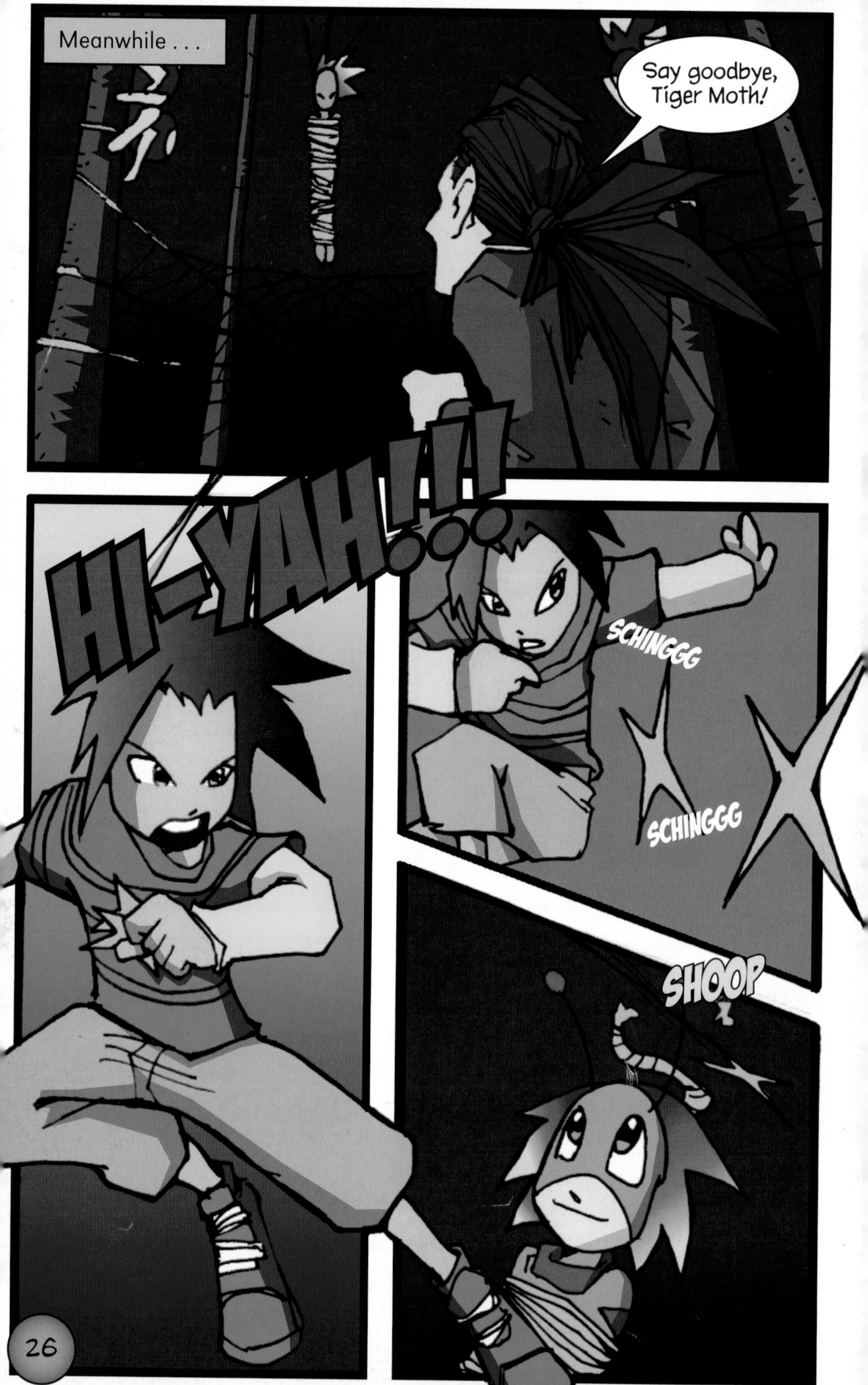
Meanwhile . . .
Say goodbye, Tiger Moth!
HI-YAH!!!!
SCHINGGG
SCHINGGG
SHOOP

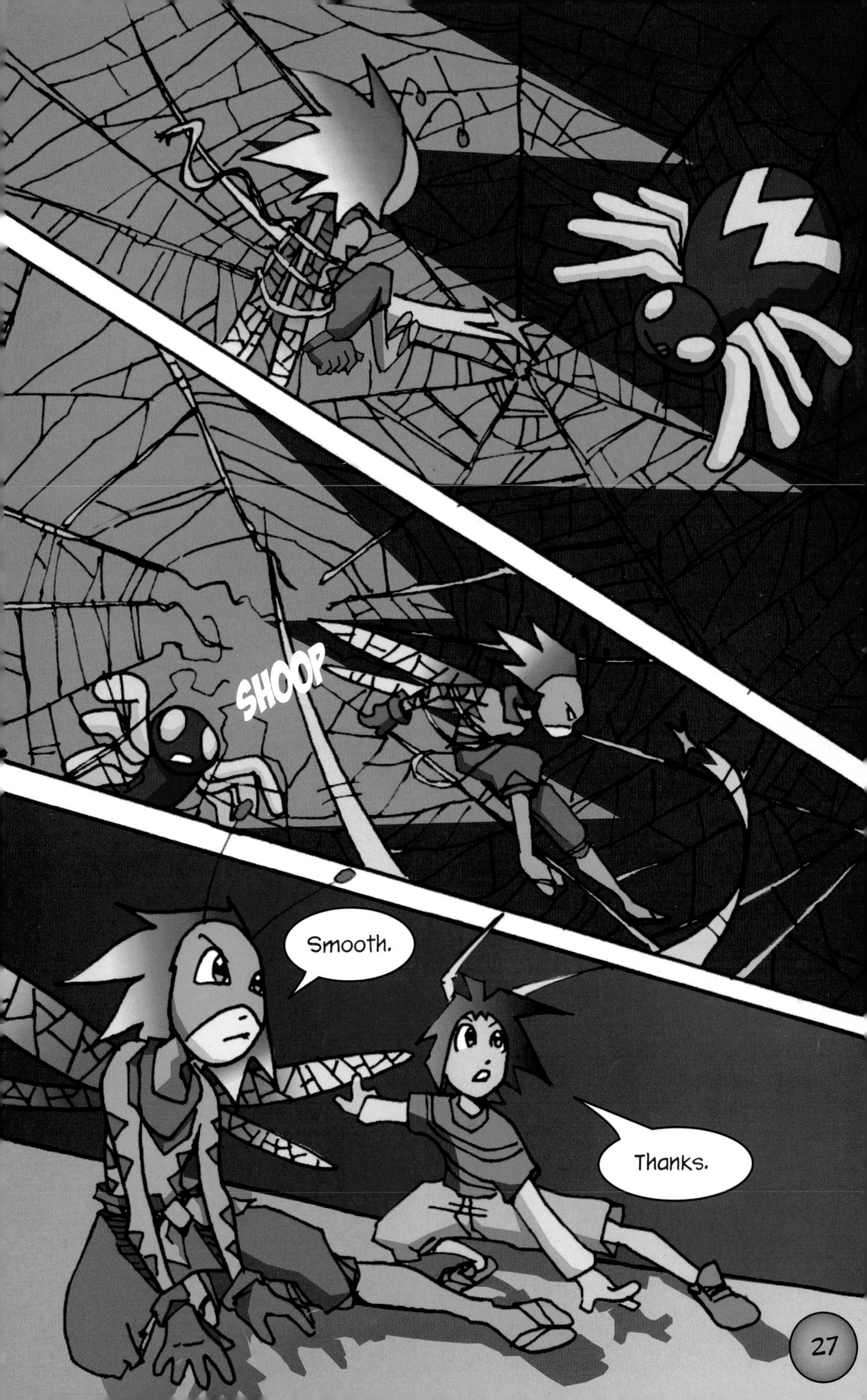
SHOOP
Smooth.
Thanks.

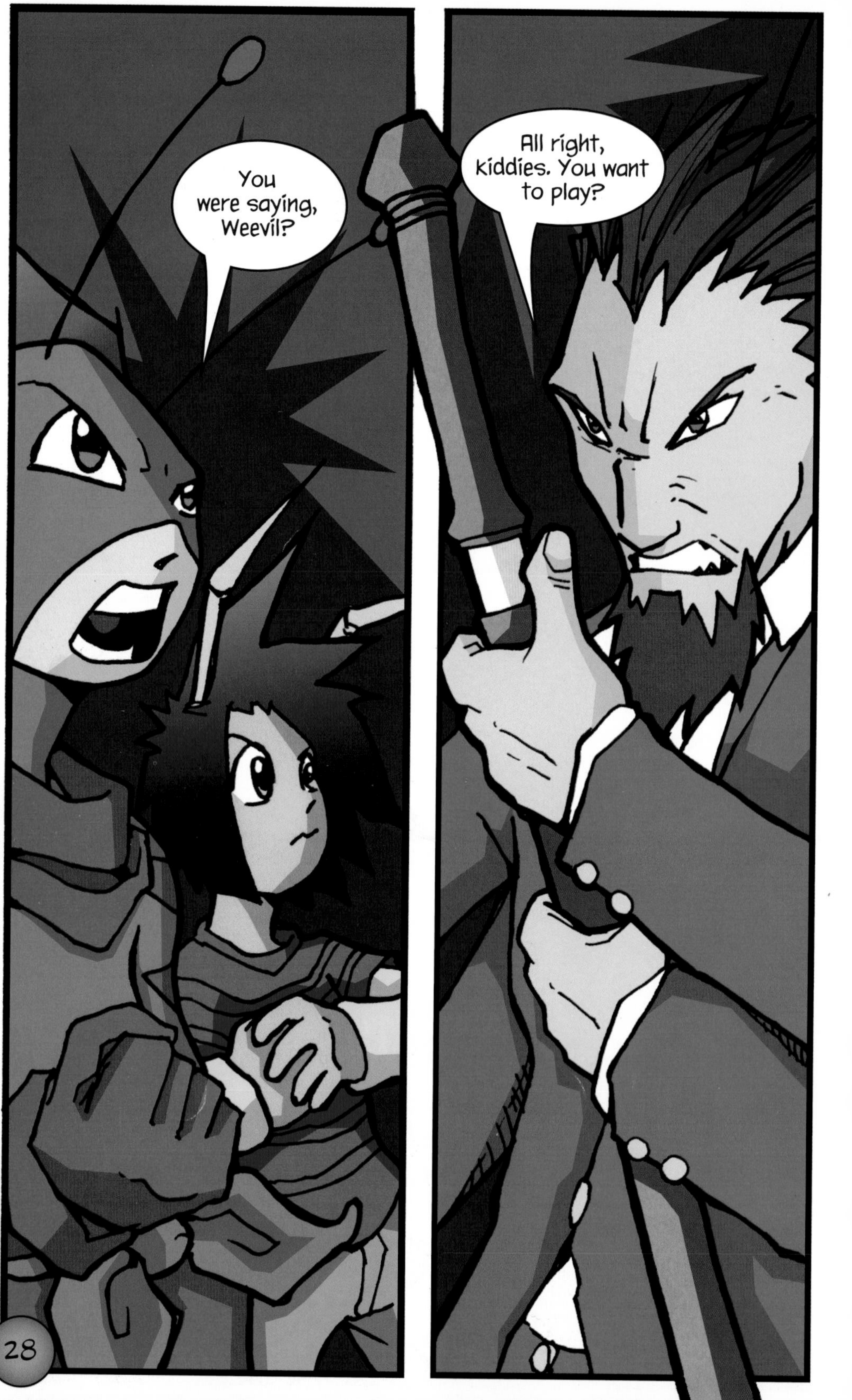
You were saying, Weevil?
All right, kiddies. You want to play?

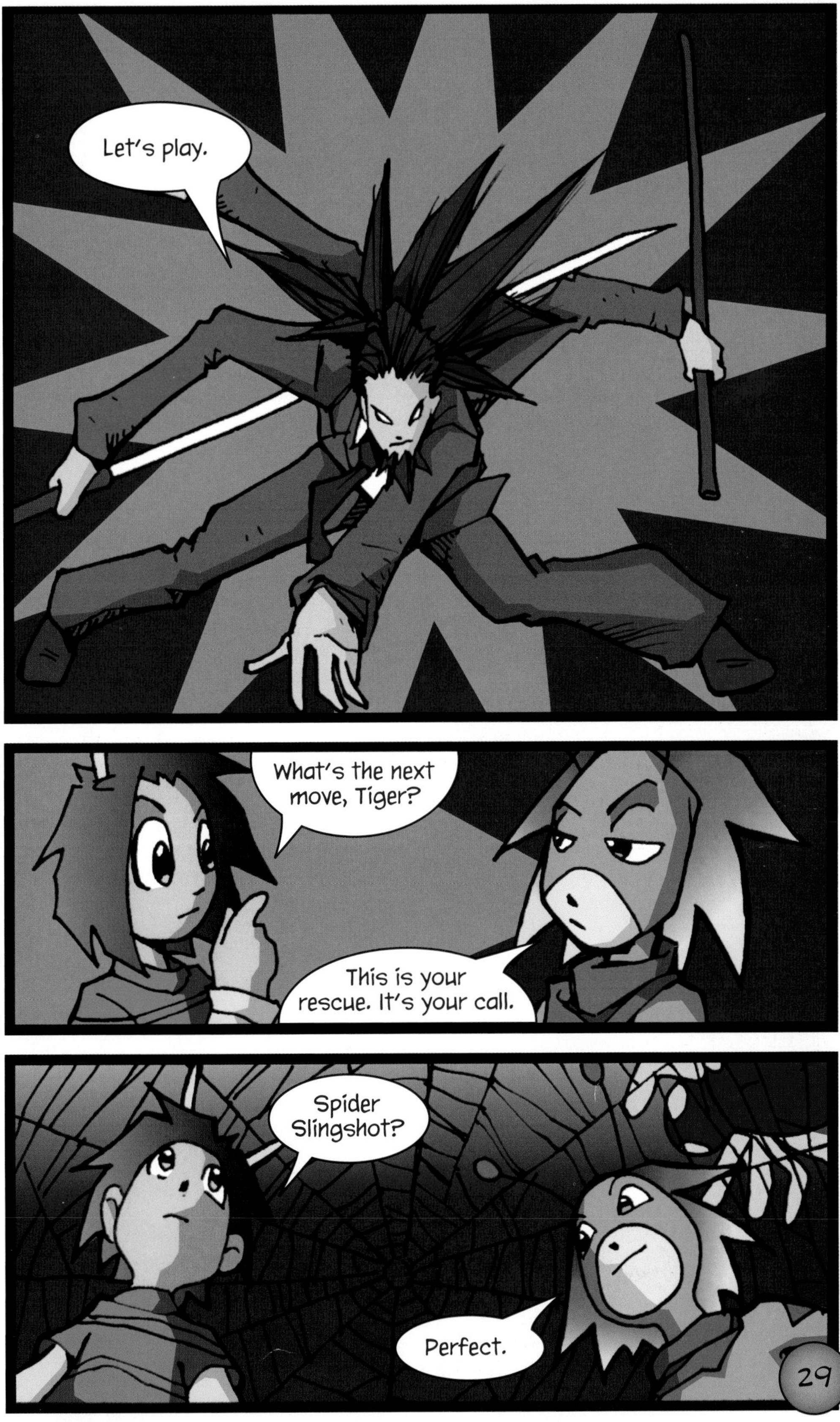
Let's play.
What's the next move, Tiger?
This is your rescue. It's your call.
Spider Slingshot?
Perfect.

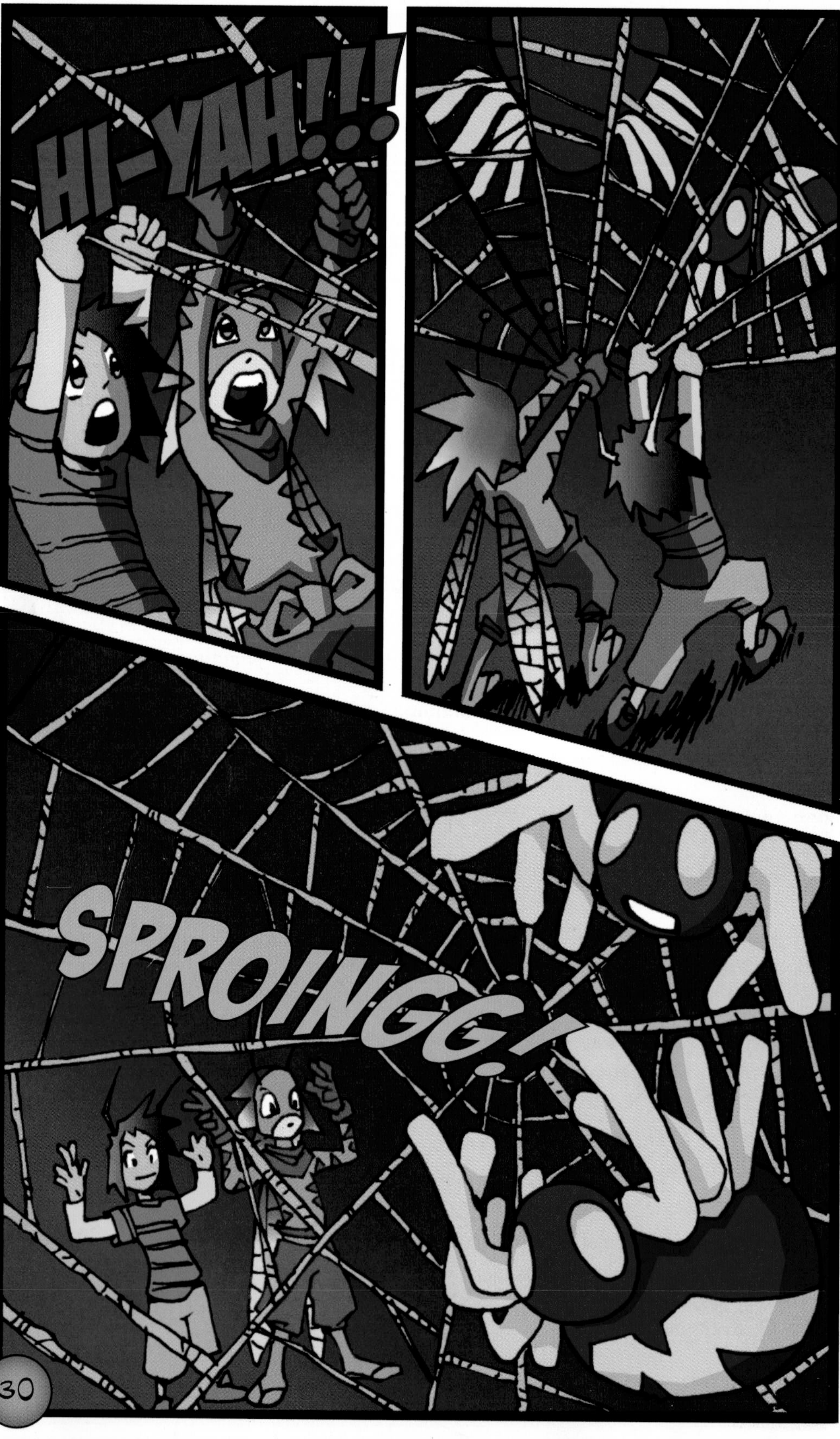
HI-YAH!!!
SPROINGG!

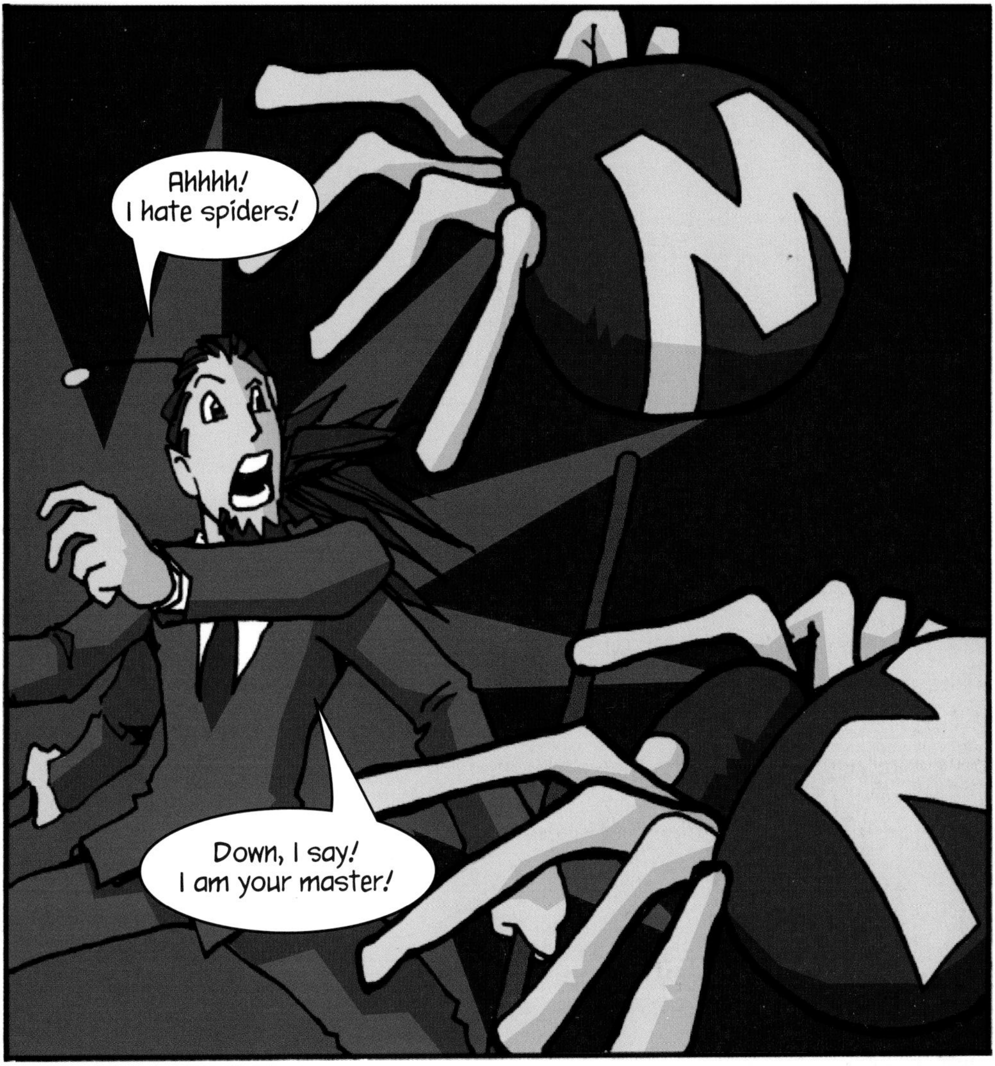
Ahhhh!
I hate spiders!
Down, I say!
I am your master!

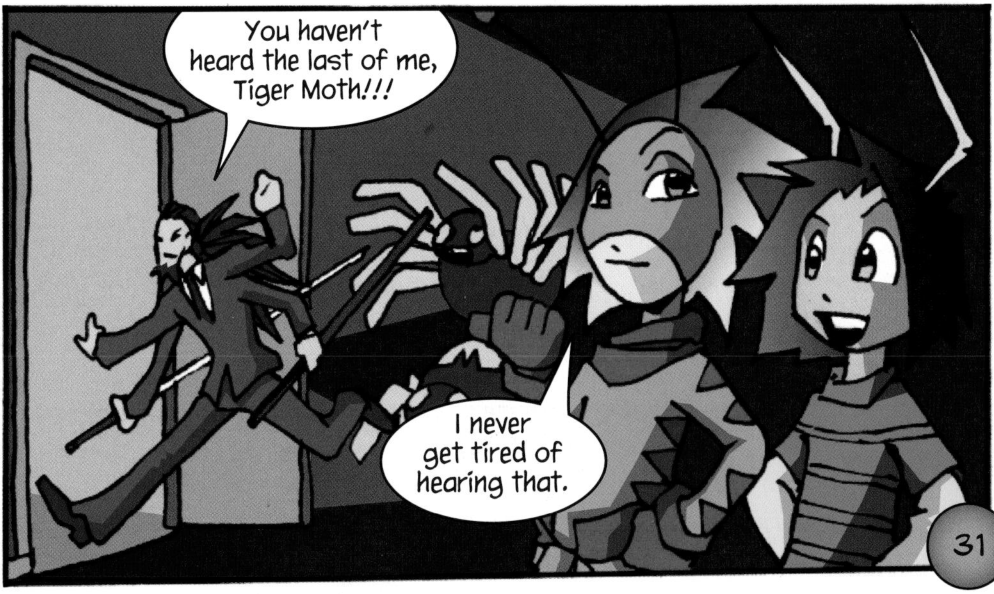
You haven't heard the last of me, Tiger Moth!!!
I never get tired of hearing that.

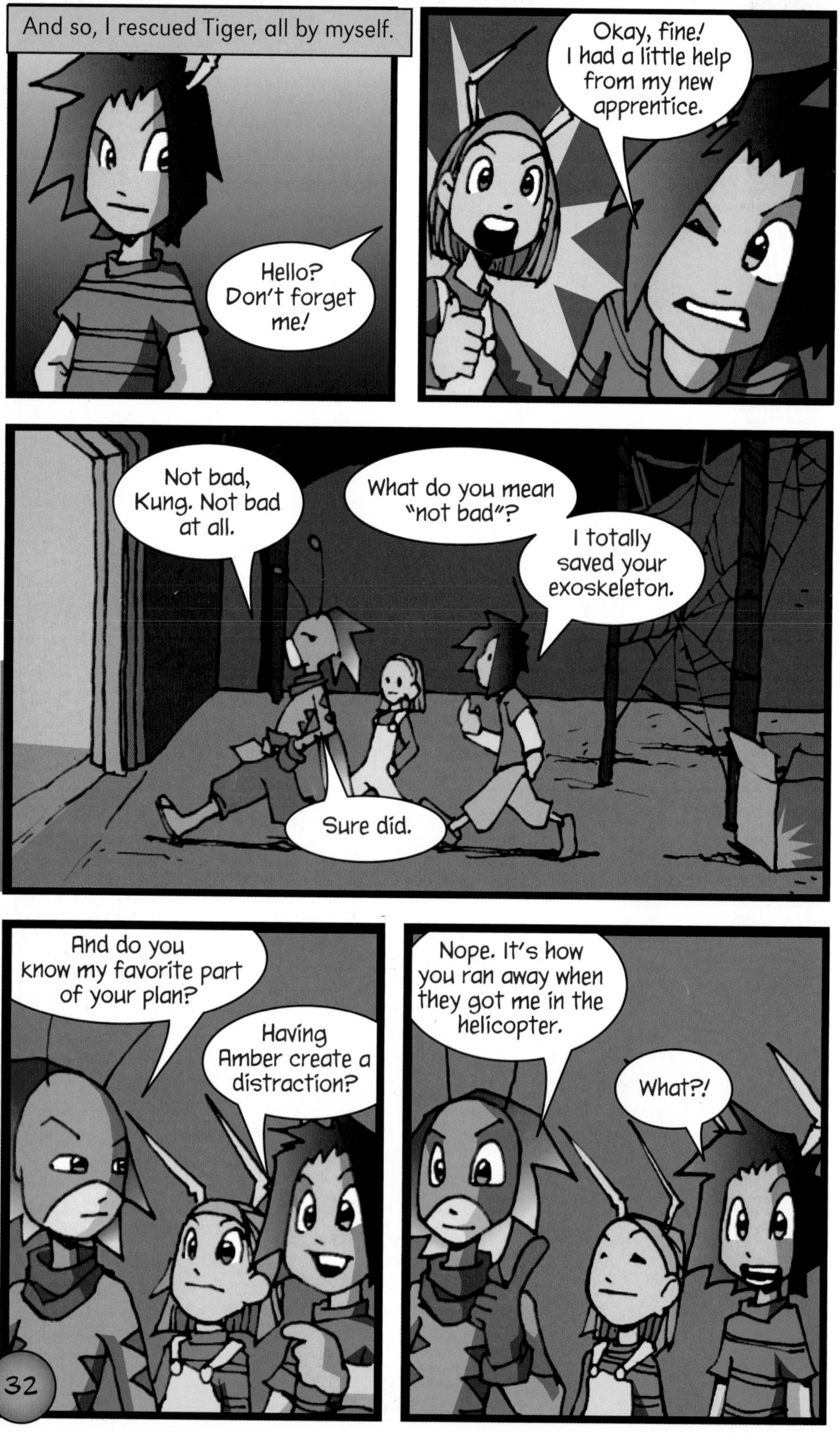
And so, I rescued Tiger, all by myself.
Hello? Don't forget me!
Okay, fine! I had a little help from my new apprentice.
Not bad, Kung. Not bad at all.
What do you mean "not bad"?
I totally saved your exoskeleton.
Sure did.
And do you know my favorite part of your plan?
Having Amber create a distraction?
Nope. It's how you ran away when they got me in the helicopter.
What?!

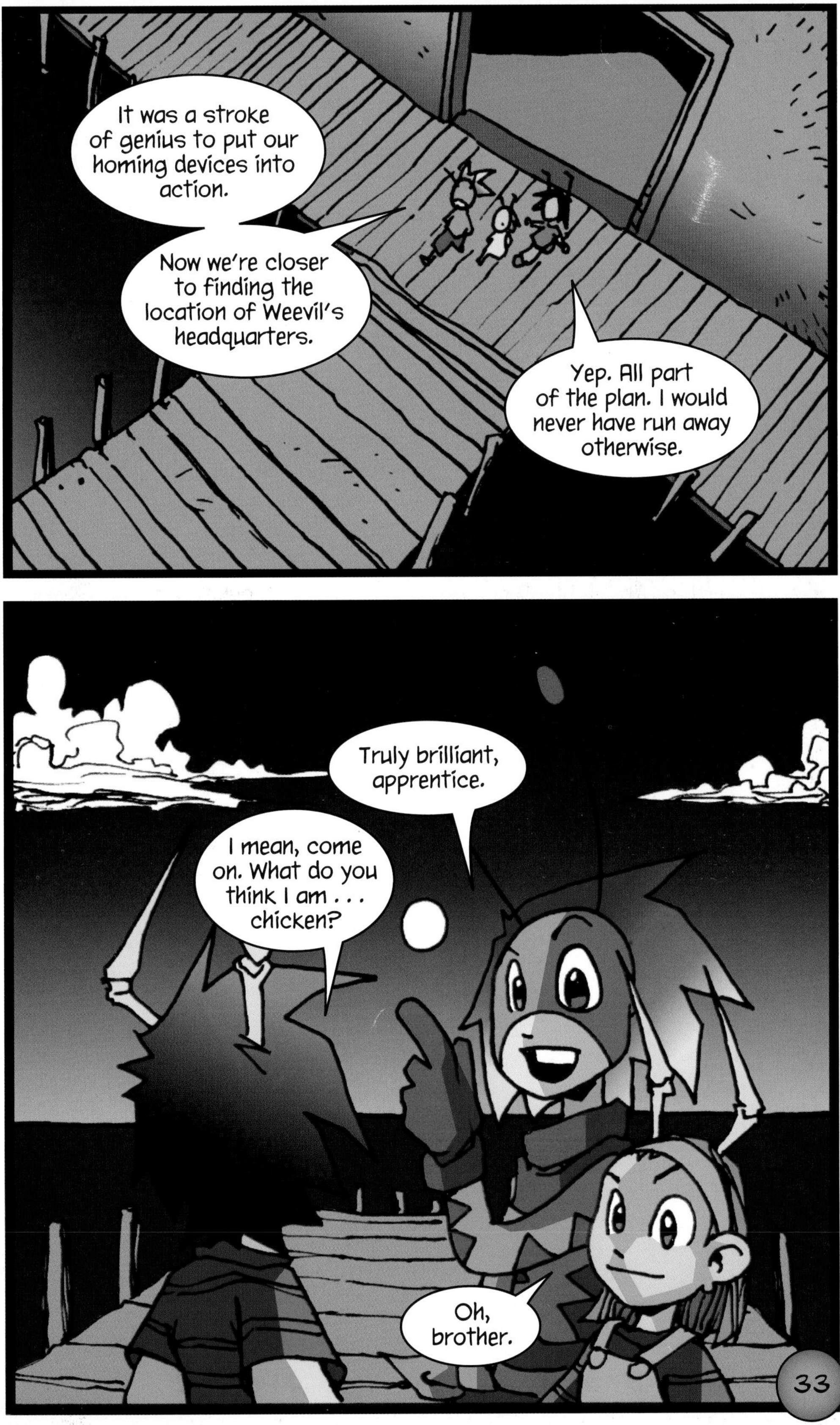
It was a stroke of genius to put our homing devices into action.
Now we're closer to finding the location of Weevil's headquarters.
Yep. All part of the plan. I would never have run away otherwise.
Truly brilliant, apprentice.
I mean, come on. What do you think I am . . . chicken?
Oh, brother.

ABOUT THE AUTHOR

Aaron Reynolds loves bugs and loves books, so Tiger Moth was a perfect blend of both. Reynolds is the author of several great books for kids, including *Chicks and Salsa,* which *Publishers Weekly* called "a literary fandango." Reynolds had no idea what a "fandango" was, but after looking it up in the dictionary (it means "playful and silly behavior"), he hopes to write several more fandangos in the future. He lives near Chicago with his wife, two kids, and four insect-obsessed cats.

ABOUT THE ILLUSTRATOR

Erik Lervold was born in Puerto Rico, a small island in the Caribbean, and has been a professional painter. Deciding that he wanted to be a full-time artist, he moved to Florida, New York, Chicago, Duluth, and finally Minneapolis. He attended the Minneapolis College of Art and Design, majored in Comic Art, and graduated in 2004. Lervold teaches classes in libraries in the Minneapolis area, and has taught art in the Minnesota Children's Museum. He loves the color green and has a bunch of really big goggles. He also loves sandwiches. If you want him to be your friend, bring him a roast beef sandwich and he will love you forever.

GLOSSARY

apprentice (uh-PREN-tiss)—a young person (or insect) that learns a skill from a more experienced person (or insect)

bamboo (bam-BOO)—a tropical plant with a woody stem

beeline (BEE-lyn)—the straightest, fastest way from one place to another

distraction (diss-TRAKT-shuhn)—something that keeps a person from thinking about what they're doing

exoskeleton (eks-oh-SKEL-uht-uhn)—the bony shell covering the outside of some insects

gizzard (GIZ-uhrd)—an inside part of a chicken or an insect. When someone says, "That sticks in my gizzard," they really mean that something bothers them.

homing device (HOHM-ing dee-VYSS)—a gadget used for locating a person or place

professional (pruh-FESH-uh-nuhl)—someone good enough at an activity to make it a career

villain (VIL-uhn)—an evil person, or bug

MORE ABOUT SPIDERS

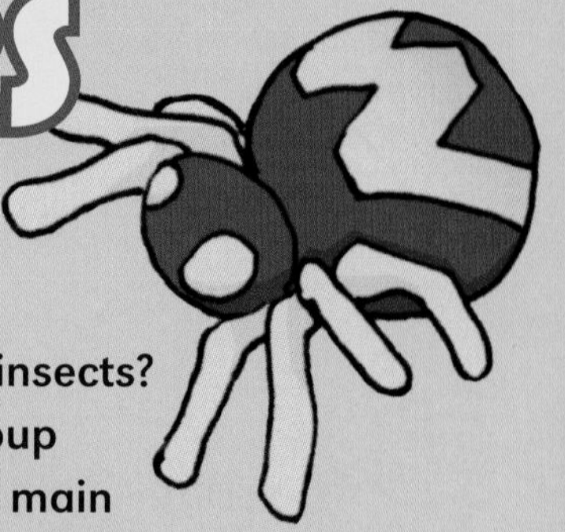

Did you know that spiders aren't actually insects? That's right. They belong to a different group called Arachnida. Most insects have three main body parts and six legs. Most spiders, on the other hand, have only two main parts to their body and eight legs.

Scientists have discovered more than 37,000 species, or different types of spiders . . . so far. They believe that possibly only 1/4 of the total number of species have been found.

The Goliath bird-eating spider is the largest spider in the world. Measuring nearly 12 inches across, this giant monster feeds on frogs, snakes, insects, lizards, and some small birds. But don't worry. Goliath bird-eating spiders are found deep within the South American rainforest and aren't very harmful to humans.

Golden orb web spiders aren't the largest spiders, but they can spin the largest webs. Often lasting for several years, their webs can stretch nearly 6 feet wide and nearly 20 feet high!

Thousands of spiders working together created the largest web ever found. According to the *Guinness Book of World Records,* money spiders built an 11.2-acre web that covered an entire high school playing field in Warwick, England.

Spiders aren't poisonous, but they are venomous. So what's the difference? Poisonous animals can be harmful if they are eaten or even touched. Venomous animals must bite or inject harmful substances into their victims.

One of the deadliest spiders in the world is the Brazilian wandering spider. This spider is also known as the banana spider because it's been found in bunches of bananas.

Spiders aren't all that bad, though. In fact, each spider eats about 2,000 bugs every year. So they actually help keep your home pest free!

Spiders can also be a tasty treat. In some Asian countries, they are seasoned and deep-fried for a roadside snack.

DISCUSSION QUESTIONS

1. Describe some of the ways Kung Pow's little sister, Amber, helped him. Do you think he could have saved Tiger Moth without her? Why or why not?

2. At the beginning of the story, Kung Pow was afraid to rescue Tiger Moth because he didn't think he was ready. Have you ever been afraid to take a test or complete a challenge? Describe the experience and how you fought through your fear.

3. Now that Kung Pow has saved Tiger Moth, do you think he's ready to battle evil bugs by himself?

WRITING PROMPTS

1. Kung Pow has learned a lot from Tiger Moth. Choose one person that you've learned a lot from, and then write a story about him or her.

2. In the end, Weevil escapes to his evil headquarters. Pretend you're the author, and write a story where Tiger Moth and Kung Pow find his hideout and take him down!

3. This Tiger Moth book was based around the character of Kung Pow. Choose your own favorite Tiger Moth character, such as the Fly Boys, Amber, Mrs. Mandible, or even Weevil, and write a story about them.

INTERNET SITES

The book may be over, but the adventure is just beginning.

Do you want to read more about the subjects or ideas in this book? Want to play cool games or watch videos about the authors who write these books? Then go to FactHound. At *www.facthound.com*, you'll be able to do all that, and more. The FactHound website can also send you to other safe Internet sites.

Check it out!